She tried not to notice the snug fit of his t-shirt as they chatted idly for several minutes, catching up on lives and acquaintances.

Finally, she had to ask. “What happened, Trip? Tell me about your accident.”

“Car crash went bad on the set.” He named one of last fall’s big blockbuster action flicks. “They edited it out completely, so you didn’t really see me on fire in the theaters.”

“On fire?” Her pulse spiked and her voice squeaked. “Oh my God!”

“Yeah.” He sounded distant, as if he didn’t like even thinking about it. “But they got me out mostly intact. Left leg was pretty much shattered, burns over most of the right, and I don’t have a spleen anymore.” She watched his chest expand as he took a deep breath. “But it could have been a hell of a lot worse. Here it is a year later and I’m up and walking. That’s more than a lot of people can say.”

There was a lump the size of a mountain in her throat, so Beth just nodded. She stuck a fried wonton in her mouth so she wouldn’t have to speak. How had he survived all that? How awful would it have been if he hadn’t? She couldn’t afford to let him back into her life, not too far, but she couldn’t imagine a world without him.

Praise for Crazy for the Cowboy, Book 2 of Love at the Crazy H, by Cindy Spencer Pape:

Five Red Roses from Red Roses for Authors Reviews:
"Cindy Spencer Pape writes a fun and entertaining, page turning story in Crazy For The Cowboy. Humorous and sensual and very romantic. A great read I highly recommend."

Four Cups from CoffeeTime Romance:
"Whew what a fantastic read. Crazy for the Cowboy has a mind-blowing beginning making this page-turner difficult to put down...Cindy Spencer Pape delivers a spellbinding read with appealing characters that enthralls. This story was so engaging it was hard to take a bathroom break."

Four and a half Quills from the Gotta Write Network:
"Crazy for the Cowboy is a wonderful addition to the Love At The Crazy H series...Pape has created another masterpiece with Crazy For The Cowboy and left this reader crazy for more!"

Four Angels from Fallen Angels Reviews:
"I read Crazy For The Cowboy in one sitting. The interplay between the two main characters is bright and often funny, and the supporting characters are all interesting as well. The plot kept me hooked, and all too soon this story ended."

Always A Cowboy

by

Cindy Spencer Pape

Thanks for Reading!
Cindy Spencer Pape

Always A Cowboy

Contact Information: info@thewildrosepress.com

Cover Art by *Tamra Westberry*

The Wild Rose Press
PO Box 708
Adams Basin, NY 14410-0706
Visit us at www.thewildrosepress.com

Publishing History
First Yellow Rose Edition, 2008
Print ISBN 1-60154-261-5

Published in the United States of America

Dedication

To Phillip B. Spencer,
because every little girl deserves a great dad,
and I've got the best.

Chapter One

"Hey Uncle Trip, wanna come play Frisbee with us?"

"Think I'll have to take a rain check on that one, Mike." Trip Hall smiled and waved his eight-year-old nephew off toward the game that was forming on the far side of the picnic area. As much as he liked the idea of a wedding reception casual enough to offer a Frisbee game, Trip was afraid his days of running through the park were behind him.

He glanced down at the ivory-handled antique cane that leaned on the picnic bench beside him. At least he'd progressed to the decorative model. That was a big improvement from the orthopedic version he'd used until recently. And he didn't even like remembering the walker or the wheelchair that had come before that. But given that less than a year ago they'd told him he'd never walk again, he didn't have much to complain about.

It was probably just this whole wedding deal that was getting him down. As of an hour ago he was officially the only unmarried Hall sibling. His oldest brother CJ had taken the plunge in February, and now middle brother Fitz had gone for a May Day wedding that apparently the whole population of the county had turned out for.

It wasn't that he wasn't happy his brothers had finally found women who could put up with them. In fact, he genuinely liked both his new sisters-in-law and had been delighted to welcome them into the family. It just felt a little weird to be the only odd man out. When he'd first moved back to Shirley last fall there had been three single brothers. "And then there was one."

"Hey stranger."

As if he'd conjured her with his thoughts, the newest member of his family sat down beside him. Heedless of her white eyelet wedding dress, Rhiannon reached down to the blanket by Trip's feet and hoisted his nine-month old son Trevor into her lap.

Trip wrapped one arm around the vibrant red-head and squeezed. "Haven't you come to your senses yet? Last chance to run away with me instead of the stiff."

Ree hugged him back and laughed at his teasing. "Nah, someone's got to make sure your uptight brother unwinds once in a while. But thanks for helping out at the store while we're on our honeymoon."

She'd recently inherited the only bookstore in the town of Shirley, Wyoming, and was almost as passionately devoted to the store as she was to Fitz. Trip and his other new sister-in-law Allie had agreed to split the workload while the newlyweds were gone, with the help of Ree's part-time assistant Lillian.

"No problem, Red. It'll be good to get out of the house a little more often. I love my new career as an author, but it gets a little lonely sometimes when the only other person around has a vocabulary limited to 'Da-da' and 'blankie'."

Ree smiled. "Good. You need to get out more. You can work on your laptop between customers, so you can keep up with your writing. And don't hesitate to take Trevor with you to the store. We moved the storeroom to the upstairs apartment and made the old one into a break room. I borrowed a playpen and a bunch of toys from Harper, so it's all set for this guy."

She bounced the giggling baby on her knee and Trip smiled. It wouldn't surprise him if she ended up using the room as a permanent day nursery in the very near future. Hell, the way things worked in his family she was probably already pregnant.

Ree wandered off with Trevor still in her arms, so Trip took advantage of the opportunity to go check out the food. Since Fitz was the county sheriff and Ree had already gotten heavily involved in local events, the wedding had been timed to kick off the town's annual spring festival. Well-wishers flooded the small city park, and nearly everyone had brought food. Three picnic tables groaned under the weight of the offerings, and Trip smiled at the panoply of sights and scents from his youth.

As he loaded his plate with Mrs. Dennison's baked

beans and Maisie Green's ambrosia salad, he caught sight of a golden blonde head over by the swings. Could it be? Back in high school, he'd only known one person with hair like that. Lizzie MacArthur had been the smartest girl in his class, and with that wheat-gold hair and big brown eyes, she'd been a natural beauty. She'd just chosen to hide it behind baggy clothes and big plastic glasses.

Could that be her pushing a little girl on the swings? There were no glasses in evidence as the woman tucked a shoulder-length strand behind her ear. The knee-length floral skirt and pink cardigan sweater were common enough to be of no help in identification.

Then he heard her laugh ring out at something the child said, and Trip was sure. Nobody laughed like Elizabeth MacArthur. It was musical and dorky at the same time—a giggle crossed with a belly laugh. The sun picked up highlights on the little girl's golden hair and coffee-colored eyes, and Trip felt a little frisson of disappointment. The child was definitely hers, no doubt about it. Oh well. They'd been just friends anyway, with nothing romantic between them. Not that Trip would have minded, but even back then Lizzie had registered as the kind of girl you didn't mess around with. She'd had serious written all over her. Trip had been in far too big a hurry to leave Shirley, Wyoming in the dust as soon as high school was over to even consider getting serious with a home-town girl. The day after graduation he'd left for the Marine Corps. And Lizzie had been headed off to college in Boulder, with a full-ride scholarship. No way would he have done anything to mess that up for her. Not after she'd been nice enough to tutor him through chemistry and trig.

But now they were obviously both grown up and back in town. He snagged a couple bottles of water out of a cooler and decided there was nothing wrong with an old friend stopping to say hello.

****

Beth Corcoran watched warily as Trip Hall approached. Tall—about six foot three now that he was done growing, she thought, and lean as ever. He was limping and it took all her willpower not to run over and take the heavy plate and bottles of water out of his hands.

She'd heard about his accident—Shirley was too small of a town for her not to—but this was the first time she'd laid eyes on him since he'd moved back home last winter. In fact, since she'd been working with Rhiannon to design a website for the bookstore, she actually knew far more about Trip—and the rest of the Hall family—than she wanted to.

"Lizzie? Is it really you?" He flashed her that mega-watt Hollywood smile which showed the one dimple in his left cheek, and handed her one of the bottles of water. After he set his plate down on a nearby stump, he held out his right hand for her to shake.

She took the water, shook his hand and smiled back, trying hard to ignore the miniscule tingle that ran up her arm at such a casual touch. Just one look in those sky-blue eyes of his had her heart going pitter-pat. She tried not to notice that his wavy black hair had been freshly trimmed, though that one rogue lock still fell across his forehead—just like it always had. She'd spent all of high school resisting the urge to smooth it back out of his face.

"It's me, all right. Though I go by Beth these days. You're looking good, Trip." And wasn't that the understatement of the year?

He shrugged, his broad shoulders rippling beneath the jacket of his western-cut suit. He and CJ had stood up with Fitz, and were all dressed up, while most of the guests were in what she called "Wyoming casual"—sweaters with denim or flowered skirts on the women, while the men wore pressed jeans and bolo ties topped by either western blazers or denim jackets.

"I'm alive. I'm walking. These days, that's about as good as I can ask for. How have you been doing, Liz—Beth?"

"Oh, I'm fine," she answered vaguely. It would be so easy to fall into those eyes and drown, to forget all the reasons she needed to steer clear of charming playboys. She chanced a look at his face, saw the new lines that bracketed his eyes, the thin white scar on his temple, and she allowed him a real smile. She was so damned glad he was here and alive. Even if he'd unintentionally broken her teenage heart, she'd never wanted him hurt. "I heard about your injuries last year. It's good to see you up and about again."

He nodded, giving her his trademark lopsided grin, the one that had haunted her dreams all through school.

"Thanks. But that's the way it goes, I guess. Life throws you curveballs and you either swing or watch them go by. And if you're smart, you learn a little something along the way. So here we are, older and hopefully wiser."

She couldn't stop the wry laugh that emerged as she nodded. "Yeah, that about sums it up, doesn't it?"

"Mommy, why'd you stop?"

Beth looked down at her almost four-year-old daughter and realized she'd quit pushing the swing. "Sorry, kiddo. Mommy was just talking to an old friend." She obediently gave Bailey's bottom another gentle shove.

"She's a beauty, just like her mom," Trip offered warmly. "What's her name?" The compliment rolled so smoothly off his practiced lips that Beth didn't think he even knew he was doing it. Trip had always been able to effortlessly charm any woman from one to one hundred. That was what made him so dangerous. She was a grown-up now, with responsibilities. She couldn't afford to fall under the hypnotic spell of Howard Hemingway Hall—better known as Triple H or Trip for short.

By now, though, Bailey was staring at the intruder with rapt curiosity. "My name's Bailey," she offered proudly. "What's yours?"

"This is Mr. Hall, honey. He went to school with Mommy a long, long time ago."

Trip laughed and gravely shook the little girl's hand, making Beth's heart twist even tighter.

"Pleased to meet you, Miss Bailey." He straightened and turned to Beth. "It sure seems that way, doesn't it? It's only been fourteen years since graduation, but it seems like a hundred."

If only he knew. Some of those years had dragged like centuries. But Beth pasted her polite social smile back in place. "I think Harper is trying to attract your attention." She pointed across the park to where Trip's oldest sister was collecting up members of the Hall family for the photographer. "It was nice seeing you again, Trip. Bye now."

He grimaced and picked up his plate. “You too, Beth. See you around sometime.” He turned and limped away.

She muttered beneath her breath, “Not if I see you first.”

****

He hadn’t been able to get her out of his mind. Lizzie—no, Beth, he reminded himself—was all grown up and even more beautiful. And she hadn’t been wearing a wedding ring. He’d gotten a little bit of information about her over the last week and a half. His sister Harper was well imbedded in the local gossip loops, and for a newcomer, his sister-in-law Allie wasn’t far behind. According to Trip’s sources, Beth, whose last name was Corcoran now, was a widow, with just the one child. Apparently she’d moved back to Shirley and taken a job at the town’s only accounting firm when her husband had passed away. Both her parents were gone now, but Trip knew that the ties of home were deep ones, and he could understand her coming back here to her roots.

And that was as far as the gossip went. Nobody seemed to know anything about Beth’s husband—who he’d been or how he’d died. The decade-plus between high school and her return to Shirley three years ago were shrouded in mystery.

He wished he could figure out why he couldn’t get her out of his mind. He’d gotten pretty damn good at avoiding old friends since he’d been back in town—so much so he’d been accused of becoming a hermit. It wasn’t like he was in the market for a relationship or anything. His own life was still way too screwed up for him to even consider the idea of dating. One thing that hadn’t changed about Beth was the vibe that screamed, “serious applicants only.”

The bell over the bookstore door chimed, and as if he’d somehow conjured her by his thoughts, Elizabeth MacArthur Corcoran walked through the door. She was dressed today in a plain navy blue suit and tailored white blouse. Her pretty, shoulder length hair was scraped back into a bun so tight it had to be giving her a headache.

Trip saved the work he’d just entered on his laptop and smiled up at her from his perch on a stool behind the counter. “Hi, Beth. Looking for something to read?”

She shook her head. “I thought Rhiannon was

supposed to be back today."

"Nope." Trip gave her a grin. "The newlyweds got back into town late last night, so they're sleeping in and unpacking today. If it's really important you can probably give her a call at the house."

"No." Her full lips compressed into a thin, worried line. "I'll come back tomorrow if you think she'll be here."

"Suit yourself. You're sure there's nothing I can help you with?"

One sensible black pump beat a tattoo on the rug. "No. It's just some design ideas for the store's website I wanted to run past her. There's no rush."

Ah. He'd caught a hint of that on the grapevine as well. She was moonlighting as a graphic designer. Given the flair she'd always had for the creative as well as her faculty with numbers, Trip was sure she was good at it.

He looked again, noticed the stress lines bracketing her mouth. He closed the lid on his laptop and slid down off the stool. His sister had Trevor today, so he could actually spend his lunch hour in adult conversation for a change. "Come on down to Benedetto's and tell me all about it. I need to set up an author website soon and I hear you're the person to talk to about that. Care to let a prospective client buy you lunch?" He picked up his cane as he walked toward the door.

Lunch at the town's one and only diner was hardly a private *tête-à-tête*, but from the look she gave him you'd have thought he'd suggested a Roman orgy. "No! I have to get back to work." She back-pedaled out the door. "Tell Ree I'll call her." The words were thrown back over her shoulder as she fled.

"Well, that went well." Trip reached down to scratch the store's resident cat, Cassius. Cass rumbled agreeably then moved back over to one of the leather couches by the gas fireplace. Trip sighed and flipped the sign on the door from "open" to "closed" then continued out to the street. Might as well go get lunch anyhow, even if it was only for himself.

****

She'd been unbelievably rude. Not to mention stupid. If she ever wanted her web design business to pay enough to be her primary source of income, she couldn't afford to turn down clients. She knew that Trip had been writing books since his accident and that the first one was due to be published soon. Of course he needed a website. And it would be a savvy business move on her part to be the one who created it. Just because she'd had a huge crush on him in high school that he hadn't returned was no reason to ignore him as an adult.

Beth hunched down in the tiny cubicle allotted to her as an assistant in Mitchell Watkins' accounting office. There would have been plenty of space to give her a real office, but that was part of Mitchell's master plan. Keep the underlings firmly tamped down. Mitchell was a hyper-conservative old goat, who really believed women belonged in the kitchen—or at the very most, manning the secretary's desk. That's part of why she was so careful to maintain her "untouchable" image in town. The slightest hint of impropriety, the least trace of gossip, and she was pretty sure Mitchell and his office manager Donna, who was just as bad, would toss Beth out on her butt. Then where would she and Bailey be?

Forcing images of Trip Hall's dimpled smile and dancing blue eyes out of her mind, she tried to concentrate on the quarterly profit statement from the local feed store. She'd only gotten halfway through it by the time she heard Mitchell and Donna leave at five.

Since Bailey was at a sleepover tonight with one of the other children from her daycare, Beth decided to stay a little longer and wrap up the task. But she was getting nowhere, so after an extra hour she threw her hands up in frustration. If she didn't get the hell out of here now, she was liable to throw her damn crappy computer monitor through the window. And that would mean the end of her job.

She packed up and decided she really needed someone to talk to—another adult for a change. Instead of going to her car, she walked down the street to the beauty shop.

"Hey there, gorgeous."

As she passed the hardware store, Len Elliot, the owner's son and heir presumptive, was just leaving. Len was average height, but his prominent beer belly made him look shorter. His mousy brown hair was already starting to recede, and maybe to compensate, he wore it too long in the back. He was Beth's age, though he'd graduated a year behind her in school, and had never married. His smile was a little too slick as he stepped out onto the sidewalk, just a bit too close for Beth's comfort. At this distance she couldn't miss the two-day stubble, or the smell of whiskey that tainted his breath. Jeez, at work, no less. She felt a moment's pity for old Mr. Elliot, who had always been kind.

"Len." She tried to step around him on the sidewalk. He stepped the same way, so they did a few awkward sidesteps until she could pass.

Len caught her elbow. "We could do this for real. There's a dance at the Moose lodge tomorrow night."

"Sorry." She shook her head and tried for a polite smile. "I've already got a date."

His dark eyes flashed like a thundercloud. "Yeah? With who?"

Like it's any of your business. She skipped ahead a step. "With my daughter. Friday night is girls' night."

It was their one ritual. Every Friday Beth and Bailey rented a movie and ate popcorn together. Bailey didn't get the concept of a ritual now, but Beth believed she was setting the tone for a closer relationship later, as Bailey grew. Beth already had the movie picked out for the next evening. It was a good thing she loved fairytales as much as her daughter did.

Len blustered something, but by then Beth had reached the sanctuary of the beauty shop and ducked inside.

"Hey Shayna, how's it going?"

Shayna Anderson, co-owner of the salon with her sister Kayla, smiled. Her corkscrew curls were an improbable shade of red this week. With her diminutive five-foot stature, she looked a little like a Raggedy Ann doll, but the overall effect was perky and cheerful. "Slow today. No more appointments either."

Beth was feeling a real need for some company and conversation—enough to splurge on eating out for a change. "You want to go grab a bite?"

Shayna's pale green eyes brightened. "Love to. And you've got perfect timing since Rick took the kids to visit his mom tonight." She gave Beth a long hard look. "Come on in and I'll give you a trim. You can pay for it by keeping me company at dinner."

"Okay." Beth really hadn't planned on a haircut, but there were certain perks that went with having your best friend from high school end up as the town hairdresser. No matter how crappy her life had been since she moved back to Shirley, thanks to Shayna, her hair always looked good.

After Shayna worked her magic, they locked up the salon and walked down the street to Benedetto's Café. Despite the Italian name, Benedetto's was a typical western diner. Ruthanne might have married a "foreigner"—her husband Tony had moved here all the way from Philadelphia, after all—but she still cooked like the farmer's daughter she was. Beth and Shayna slid into a corner booth and gave their orders to Ruthanne's daughter Becky, then sat back with tall frosty glasses of iced tea to catch up.

"Saw you leaving the bookstore today," Shayna mentioned. "Is Ree back from her honeymoon?"

"Back in town but not at the shop until tomorrow, according to Trip."

"Nice of him to help out while she was gone." Shayna took a long pull of her iced tea. "It's good to see him around town a little more often, even if he does still have the cane."

It was. Beth couldn't argue with that, but she also couldn't explain to her friend that she wished *she* didn't have to run into him. Shayna had never understood Beth's massive crush on Trip, and Beth sure as heck didn't want to explain it to her now. She really didn't want to think about the way being around Trip made her feel—the fact that he woke up urges she'd thought were long dead.

Why couldn't she stop thinking about him? He was just another old friend, nothing more. So why did all her senses jump to alert when she saw his sister Harper Dargitz walk in, her husband and brood of children following her? Just because the Hall clan tended to gather in groups?

Beth watched, as they moved tables to make a big

enough space, and she breathed a sigh of relief when Trip wasn't with them. She waved to Harper and Jim, then to CJ and Allison Hall when they entered and joined them, but ignored the odd speculative glances Shayna kept throwing her.

Chapter Two

By the time dinner was over, she'd chastised herself enough, felt guilty enough, that she knew she had to go talk to Trip, apologize for being so curt in the bookstore today. Shayna had told her he was living in his grandparents' old place. Making things right between them was the smart business move, she rationalized as she drove out of town. It was also the polite, neighborly thing to do. It had nothing to do with his smile or his sexy blue eyes. Nope. Nothing.

She knew the way to his grandparents' log-cabin style home. The crowd had come out here from time to time to swim in the pond his grandfather Ryan had so carefully maintained. Beth's mom had been on a couple of church committees with Trip's grandma, too, and Beth had come along on the occasional visit.

She parked her compact station wagon next to a shiny silver, new-model SUV with a temporary handicapped permit hanging from the mirror. She bet Trip hated that. His leg must be worse than it had looked at the picnic if he was willing to admit to weakness to that extent. She swallowed her trepidation and mounted the front steps, still trying to decide what she was going to say. Inhaling through her nose, she squared her shoulders and knocked.

"Come on in, it's open." His sinfully deep voice penetrated the heavy wooden door. She turned the handle and stepped inside.

Cabin described the architectural style, but not the size or elegance of the comfortable two-story home. The first thing she noticed was that he'd redecorated. Instead of his grandmother's frilly Victorian style, the room now looked like the main lounge at an exclusive wilderness lodge. Large, comfortable-looking furniture was covered in brown leather that looked buttery soft, and framed

Audubon prints graced the walls. A portable crib and baby swing sat near the sofa, and a big pile of toys cluttered one corner. A laptop computer was open on the coffee table. She took all this in almost automatically, with the bulk of her attention focused on the man in front of her, who was sprawled in a recliner with his leg up, and his back to the door. There was a diaper bag and a pile of trash on the floor beside the chair.

"Thanks for coming," his voice sounded taut, stretched. "Can you get the TV remote? It fell on the floor beside the coffee table."

"What?" Her voice cracked, damn it. Did he think she was some kind of servant, or one of his Hollywood groupies?

His head spun around. "Who… Beth? What the hell are you doing here? I was expecting Harper."

Beth moved around the chair so she could see him, and he could see her without breaking his neck. He wore ragged grey sweatpants and a Marine Corps sweatshirt that had definitely seen better days, and he held a squirming baby in his lap.

"Harper was still eating dinner when I left Benedetto's."

"Oh. She didn't say she was in town." The baby's motions grew more and more restless as they stared at each other. Every time he bounced, she saw Trip wince. "Look, I hate to ask, but could you please grab the remote off the floor? The little guy wants music, and my voice just doesn't do it for him."

Beth could imagine. Trip was incredible at a lot of things, but he never could carry a tune in a bucket. She walked over to the table and picked up the remote, then turned around and handed it to Trip. He clicked on *Sesame Street*, then sighed when his son immediately stilled. "Thank you, God," he whispered. Then he looked back up at Beth. "Do you think you could put him in the bouncer? He'll be happy in there for the next twenty minutes or so. By then, my pain meds should have kicked in."

Pain meds? He did look awfully pale. "No problem." She reached out and lifted the little guy, gulping when he immediately snuggled against her chest. She missed having a baby to hold now that Bailey was older. She was absolutely not going to think about how wonderful he smelled, of fruit, and talc, and something unidentifiably sweet. Once the baby was installed in his bouncy chair watching the widescreen TV, she turned back to Trip.

"What's wrong?"

"Right now or in general?" He was gritting his teeth around the words, his lips a thin white line.

"Now."

"Muscles spasms in the calf and thigh. I guess I overdid it a little in physical therapy today."

"How long since you took the pain pills?"

He squeezed his eyes shut. "Haven't gotten to them yet. Had to get Trevor settled first."

Trevor. Nice name. And damn, if she didn't admire Trip's priorities. "Where are they?"

He pointed to the kitchen. "Cabinet over the sink. The one with the baby-lock on it."

She went to the cabinet, found several prescription bottles, and read them. Two were pain medications. "Which one? The ibuprofen or the oxycodone?"

"Ibuprofen for now. I'm trying to avoid the narcotics as much as possible. Once Harper gets here to watch Trevor, I'll take a muscle relaxant. They knock me out a little bit."

"Take it now. I'll stay till she gets here." Where had that offer come from? Still, she found that bottle, and shook one of those tablets out along with the ibuprofen. Without even thinking, she reached into the cupboard where Mrs. Ryan had always kept the glasses. She pulled one out, filled it up from the sink, and took it to him along with the meds. "Here."

"Thanks." He took the pills, swallowing half the glass of water in one slug. Then he looked up at her with narrowed eyes. "Not that I'm not grateful, but just what the hell are you doing here?"

She grimaced. "I came to apologize."

He couldn't believe that Beth was standing here in his living room. For fourteen years, he'd wondered what had happened to her, but they'd never crossed paths in all that time. He was getting tired of looking up at her, though, and he was humiliated that he couldn't even stand up to look her in the eyes. He gestured toward the chair beside him. "Sit. Please."

She lowered herself primly into the chair, ankles neatly crossed, and spine erect. Her hands were folded in her lap. He'd always gotten a kick out of her ladylike manner, gotten an even bigger kick when he could make her laugh and lose it. But that was a long time in the past, and right now he hurt too much to even think about it.

"Apologize for what?"

"For running out of the bookshop like the devil was on my heels. It's just that Mitchell gets so crabby if I'm even a second late from my lunch hour, and I had other errands to run."

He wasn't buying it, not completely. There was something else in her reaction, but he wasn't up to figuring it out right now. He waved a hand. "Don't sweat it. I heard you were widowed, Beth. I want to tell you I'm sorry for your loss. And your mom. She died while I was in the service, I think." Beth's father had passed away while they were still in high school.

"Thanks. And you too. I don't think you knew, but I was at your father's funeral. You were so caught up with everything that I didn't want to intrude, but I was here visiting Shayna that week and wanted to pay my respects. Both he and your mother were good people." She gestured around the room, and her voice thickened. "Your grandparents, too. God, I can't believe how much has changed in the last fourteen years."

"Everything changes. Even us. You're looking good, kiddo. And your little girl is a heartbreaker."

She ignored the complement to herself, he noticed, but preened a little when he praised her daughter.

"So is the little guy over there. And you're doing pretty well from what I hear, with your new career as a mystery writer. Are you just here to regroup, or are you staying this time?"

"Staying." Nothing short of a nuclear blast could get him to go back to Los Angeles. "I want Trevor to grow up around his cousins. Shirley's a good place to raise a kid."

Beth nodded her agreement, then tipped her head at Trevor. "How old is he?"

"Nine months and a bit." Trip smiled. He'd been unsure about being a father when he'd first learned about Trevor, but now he couldn't imagine a life without his son. The drugs must have begun to kick in because Beth was starting to fuzz around the edges.

"Where's his mom?"

Her words seemed to come from a long way away. *Whose mom? Oh Lorelei.* "Dead," he muttered. He barely heard her response as he leaned back into the chair and let sleep overcome him.

****

Dead? Oh, man, that sucked. Beth had first-hand experience with just how much. She wondered if Trip's wife/girlfriend had been killed in the same accident where he'd gotten hurt. Or maybe she'd died in childbirth. Either way, he'd had one hell of a tough year, poor guy.

She looked over at Trip to ask more questions, but realized his head had fallen back against the chair. Wow, the muscle relaxant apparently did knock him out. And he'd always slept like a rock. A soft snore escaped him, and Beth smiled, remembering one time he'd fallen asleep on the bus during a school trip. She and Shayna had painted his toenails pink while he snored.

A nasty smell assailed her nostrils, and she looked around for the source. *Ah.* The pile of trash at Trip's side was a dirty diaper. He'd probably been in too much pain to get up and throw it away, but he'd made sure his son was comfortable. Damn, she wasn't supposed to admire the man who'd broken her heart. Beth picked the diaper up between two fingers and carried it to the garbage can in the kitchen. Then, deciding it was too stinky to leave in the house, she tied up the trash bag and set it outside the back door, before rummaging under the sink for a fresh bag. Mission accomplished, she ducked back into the living room to check on Trevor, who was still chortling along with Elmo.

Hmm, now what? Trip had called his sister, but Beth had no idea how long it would be before Harper arrived. Restless, she tidied the pile of toys, then carried a few dirty dishes out to the kitchen. The house was clean, she discovered, just a little cluttered with baby stuff. She rinsed the dishes and put them into the dishwasher, wishing she'd brought some work, or a book, or something else to do. Returning to the living room, she sat down and tried to watch Sesame Street with Trevor.

It wasn't holding her attention. Her gaze wandered to the coffee table and the laptop. No, that would be snooping, she decided. There was a book lying next to it, though. A paperback with a plain blue cover. "Advance Reading Copy," she read out loud. Then she saw the rest. "*Murder on the Set*, by H. H. Hall."

Half an hour later, Trip was still asleep, and Beth was engrossed in the book. Who knew Trip could write? The hero was a stuntman who got caught up investigating a series of killings during a movie shoot. When Trevor had tired of Sesame Street and started to cry, Beth had simply picked him up and plopped him on her lap, then begun reading out loud in a soft murmuring tone, like she used to do with Bailey. She skipped over a few swear words, though he wouldn't know what the words meant, anyway. A few minutes later, Trevor was as soundly asleep as his father, and Beth was still reading.

Beth jumped as the front door swung open and Trip's sister Harper bustled in. "Sorry it took me so long, but I had to take Rainey to soccer practice."

"Sshh." Beth held a finger in front of her mouth. "They're both out like lights."

Harper's jaw dropped open, but to give her credit, she didn't shriek. "What are you doing here?"

"Right now, reading a really good book," Beth answered, just as quietly. "I came up to talk about designing his web site, but he wasn't feeling up to it. Trip took a muscle relaxant about thirty minutes ago. I told him I'd keep an eye on Trevor till you got here."

"O-o-okay." Harper gaze was openly speculative.

Beth eased Trevor into a different position against her chest so she could stand. She walked over to Harper and handed her the baby. "Here. Tell Trip I'll bring the book back tomorrow."

****

He still couldn't wrap his head around the fact that Lizzie—no, he had to remember to think of her as Beth—MacArthur—*arrgh, what was her last name now?*—had been in his home last night.

And he'd passed out, right in front of her.

Way to go, Hall.

Trip flexed his knee, did another few reps on the weight bench in his basement. The machine was set to damn near the minimum, and it was still all he could do to finish a set. The baby monitor on the crate next to him was yet another reminder of how the mighty had fallen in the space of a single year.

Not, he reminded himself, that he'd change everything. He loved being a dad, even if he hadn't planned on it quite yet, or on doing it solo. But Trevor was far and away the best thing in his life, the reason he'd fought so hard to walk again, to build a new career that didn't depend on muscle tone and reflex speed.

And now it was happening. His leg was improving. He had his own home, a supportive family, and his first book due out in just over a month. He had the sequel almost ready to send to his editor and enough money in the bank to see things through if the book flopped. In the grand scheme of things, he didn't have much to complain about.

Except the raging case of lust he'd woken up with after dreaming about Beth. Where had that come from? He'd never looked at her that way before. Had he? He damn sure wasn't in any position to do anything about it now.

After last night's muscle spasm, Trip didn't dare work the leg too hard, so he sat up and switched the machine to bench presses, then loaded on the weight. He had to work off this frustration somehow, and pumping iron was one of the few socially acceptable ways to do it. He'd given up hard liquor and tobacco since he'd gotten Trevor, so Scotch and cigars were out of the question.

Harper had given him an earful about not overdoing it when he'd woken up last night. Big sister was more than a bit protective of her chicks, and as the baby of the Hall family, Trip still qualified, even though Harper now had four kids of her own. Plus, he knew he'd given the whole family a hell of a scare last year when he'd spent almost two months in a coma, then wound up with Trevor before he was even fully on his feet.

As soon as he'd been able, he'd packed up and headed

home, staying with CJ at the ranch. That had lasted till Allie showed up at Christmastime. Sharing a house with a pair of brand-new lovebirds wasn't Trip's idea of a good time. So he'd opened up the house his grandparents left him, arranged for a house-keeper/babysitter, and hunkered down to write books and raise his son.

Most of the time it worked. Incidents like last night didn't happen often, and when it did, either Teresa Ryan, his housekeeper, would come back and watch Trevor, or one of his siblings would come over. He hated being dependent, but his pride took a back seat to his son's safety. Still the whole situation did give his siblings, especially Harper, leverage for treating him like an infant himself sometimes. Trip understood, and he tried to cut them some slack, but that didn't mean he liked it.

His mind kept wandering back to Beth. Why was he so hung up on someone he hadn't seen since the day they graduated high school? He hadn't really been interested in sex since the accident, so why was his libido coming back now, all at once. Was it just a sign that his body was healing? He didn't think so, since the change seemed directly related to Beth. Why did just the thought of her make him as randy as a lovesick eighteen year old?

****

After work, Beth picked up Bailey from the pleasant home daycare center and realized she was too wiped out to cook. Shirley boasted a few restaurants, none of which were very expensive, so she decided to splurge on take-out. Eating someone else's cooking two nights in a row—what was her world coming to? Maybe Shayna was right—maybe she did need to get a life. Or maybe just talking to Trip Hall turned her world upside down.

Whichever it was, she stopped at June's Korean, which had evolved into a sort of pan-Asian jumble. June Johnson—it had originally been Yun—had come to Shirley as a Korean war bride, and her descendants still ran the place with one rule—give the customers what they want. The menu boasted a wide range of Sino-American dishes as well as a few traditional Korean ones. That worked out well for Beth since she liked *bibimbap* and Bailey had a passion for sweet and sour chicken.

As she waited in line, Beth's cell phone rang. The

caller was unidentified but the number was local, so she answered. “Hello?”

“Hello, Beth? This is Trip Hall. Ree gave me this number and said it was the best way to reach you about your website design business.”

“Oh. Hi, Trip. How’s the leg today?” She shooed Bailey over toward a child-sized table in the corner where coloring books and crayons could be found.

“Much better. Thanks again for helping out last night. And sorry about passing out on you.”

She waved a hand even though she knew he couldn’t see it. “No problem, glad I could help. You said you called about your website?”

“Yeah, when would be a good time for you to get together and discuss it?”

“Have you eaten?”

What? The question had popped out before she’d even known she was going to say it. She felt like crawling under the counter. *Please let him say no!*

“No, I could meet you someplace.”

Damn it! She swallowed hard. She was in for it now. “You still like June’s *bulgogi*?”

“Mmmm. Heaven in a white cardboard box.”

“If you don’t mind my bringing Bailey with me, I’ll grab the food and come up now. We can go over the basics.”

“Sure, she can watch a video or something if that’s all right.”

She hung up and added a significant chunk of food to her order. She was wining and dining a client right? That made it deductible, she reasoned. The accountant in her made sure she carefully tucked the receipt into her wallet. She hefted her order, collected Bailey, and headed up a mountain for the second time in as many days.

****

Trip hated editing, but it was an important part of the writing process. That’s what he kept telling himself. In truth, he was doing re-writes because his brain wasn’t functioning well enough to write anything new.

Teresa knocked at the door of Trip’s home office. “You sure it’s okay if I leave early?”

“It’s fine,” he assured her. Teresa was a nice woman

in her early fifties. Her kids were grown and her husband was a long-haul trucker, so he was gone a lot. In exchange for working the occasional evening, she sometimes left early when Steve was home. "I'm not getting anywhere with this today anyway. Might as well play with the kid."

Teresa smiled. "He's asleep, but probably not for much longer. He was a little crabby earlier, probably has another tooth coming in."

Yeah, teething was fun. "Teething toys are in the freezer, right?" The little gel-filled rings seemed to help.

"Right. And there's some leftover lasagna in the fridge for your dinner. Don't forget to eat."

"I promise I'll have dinner." He grinned, holding up three fingers in a Boy Scout salute. For some reason he didn't want to mention that Beth was on her way with take out. "Now go. Have a hot night on the town with your husband."

She snorted. "In Shirley? You've got to be kidding!" But she was heading toward the door as she said it.

Moments later, Trip heard the front door shut and her car start up.

He stood and stretched, testing the leg as he did so. So far, so good today. He walked into the other downstairs bedroom, currently set up as a playroom for Trevor. The little guy was still napping, so Trip wandered out to the living room and turned on the TV. Five minutes into Sports Center, Beth and Bailey knocked on his front door, bearing a briefcase and a steaming paper sack.

Trip held the door while they stepped inside.

Beth, looking all prim and proper in a tan skirt and jacket over a yellow Oxford-style shirt, handed him the paper bag. "I hope you're hungry."

His stomach growled, answering for him. The scents coming from the sack were heavenly. "Thanks."

"How's your leg today?"

"Fine. Last night wasn't normal. Usually I get around the house just fine." He set the bags down on the table and brushed his hair back out of his eyes. "I'll get some plates."

The living room and kitchen were really one large space, so he didn't have very far to go. She was watching him, though. He could feel her eyes on his back, taking stock of his limp as he moved.

"There's iced tea in the fridge." He spoke over his shoulder as he gathered plates, glasses, and napkins. Unless Beth had changed even more than he'd noticed, she preferred chopsticks to forks.

Bailey helped her mom pull cardboard cartons from the sack. Bless Beth, she'd brought enough to feed an army. Or an eighteen-year-old boy, which was of course how she remembered him. Trip found a Denver phone book and set it on one of his kitchen chairs then covered it with a towel for the little girl. Harper had a daughter not too much younger, so he knew the drill. He gave Bailey an easy grin and helped her into the chair while he asked her mother. "You treat all your potential customers to dinner?"

"Well, I also had to return your book," she admitted with a familiar flush. She always had blushed easily, and it always had been fun to make her do it. "I kind of found it on the table after you fell asleep last night, and I took it home to finish it."

His book? She'd read his book? Damn, now he was probably the one blushing.

"It's good, Trip, *really* good. I never knew you could write."

He gestured for her to sit, and eased himself into the chair across from her. "Neither did I." He poured tea for the adults and milk for Bailey while Beth filled her daughter's plate with rice and chicken with just a tiny bit of sauce. Then Trip helped himself to some *bulgolgi* while Beth piled a heap of rice onto her own plate. When they switched cartons, it went just as smoothly as if they did this every day.

"I started screwing around with it during downtime on the sets. Then when I was in the hospital, I needed something to keep my mind occupied so I didn't go bug-nuts. My former stunt agent has a friend with a literary agency, and the rest just sort of happened."

Beth shook her head and rolled her eyes. Trust Trip to downplay his own achievements. "I don't believe that. That book was too good to just happen." A lot of thought and care had gone into crafting that gripping tale of suspense laced with self-deprecating humor.

She tried not to notice the snug fit of his t-shirt as they chatted idly for several minutes, catching up on lives and acquaintances.

Finally, she had to ask. "What happened, Trip? Tell me about your accident."

"Car crash went bad on the set." He named one of last fall's big blockbuster action flicks. "They edited it out completely, so you didn't really see me on fire in the theaters."

"On fire?" Her pulse spiked and her voice squeaked. "Oh my God!"

"Yeah." He sounded distant, as if he didn't like even thinking about it. "But they got me out mostly intact. Left leg was pretty much shattered, burns over most of the right, and I don't have a spleen anymore." She watched his chest expand as he took a deep breath. "But it could have been a hell of a lot worse. Here it is a year later and I'm up and walking. That's more than a lot of people can say."

There was a lump the size of a mountain in her throat, so Beth just nodded. She stuck a fried wonton in her mouth so she wouldn't have to speak. How had he survived all that? How awful would it have been if he hadn't? She couldn't afford to let him back into her life, not too far, but she couldn't imagine a world without him.

"So tell me about you, Beth. You headed off to college all full of big plans. What brought you back to Shirley?"

She shrugged. Desperation was the real answer, but she wasn't ready to admit to that. "It was home. A place to start over after…" she tipped her head toward Bailey. "After Daniel passed."

Trip nodded. "How'd that happen?"

"Pneumonia." She didn't have any desire to elaborate, explain that Daniel's habits and habitual dissipation had been at the root of his illness.

"I'm sorry."

She shrugged. "It's been three years. You move on."

"I guess you do. Nobody else in the picture?"

"No." She didn't want to go down this road, so she took another gambit. "How about you? Were you married to Trevor's mother?"

"No. She ditched me while I was in the coma. Told

my brothers she didn't want to be tied to a vegetable, and split." His whole face shuttered. "She never bothered to tell them—or me—that she was pregnant. I would have never even known about Trevor if she hadn't died. The only favor she ever did me was putting my name on his birth certificate."

Whoa! That was a lot of information to process in a hurry. She swallowed the last of her tea and nodded in agreement. "That's awful." She didn't ask if Trip was sure the baby was his. One look last night had told her that much. Hall genes ran awfully true. "How'd she die?"

"Car accident. She'd been drinking. If Trevor hadn't been strapped into his car seat in the back, she'd have probably taken him with her."

Beth bit down a wave of nausea. That's awful! How could any mother risk her child like that?"

Trip shook his head, all the laughter gone from his eyes. "I have no idea."

There was silence for a few awkward moments, Finally Beth swallowed and asked, "How long has he been with you?"

"Since I got out of the hospital in November. Harper and her youngest stayed with me in California to look after him till I was on my feet and ready to move back here."

"Well, he's a lucky kid."

"How do you figure that?"

"He's a Hall." She waved her chopsticks in an airy motion. "It's like being born with a membership in the world's most exclusive 'I've got your back' club. Do you have any idea how much I would have given to be part of a family like yours?"

He shrugged, a classic Trip Hall gesture. "It never even occurred to me. Back in high school, I'm not sure I considered being the baby of the Hall family a good thing. It was awfully hard to get away with anything when I had four older siblings watching me all the time."

"I remember." It was time to lighten things up, quickly. She rolled her eyes and gave him a look she knew he'd interpret as "men are so stupid."

"When I was hurt though—they really rallied around me. Took turns staying with me while I was in the hospital. The first week they were all there—though I wasn't conscious to remember it. I think that was a big part of why the judge was so quick to grant me custody. He said I had a great support system that boded well for the baby, even if I never fully recovered."

"Mommy, I have to go potty." Bless Bailey for interrupting a conversation that had grown all too personal.

"You remember where?" Trip asked Beth.

She nodded. "Down the hall to the left, right?"

"Right. Left." He grinned back, then turned to Bailey. "Would you like to watch *Finding Nemo* or *Winnie the Pooh* after dinner? I'll get it set up for when you come back."

"Nemo," Bailey replied. She took Beth's hand and skipped happily with her down the hall, clearly taken with the man who spoke so politely to her and smiled. But then, her mother thought sourly, what woman wasn't?

****

Trevor had demanded his dinner while Beth was with Bailey in the restroom, so Trip was feeding his son when the two females returned. He had to smile when he saw the little girl's eyes go wide at the sight of the younger child.

"Bailey, this is my son, Trevor."

"He's a baby." Her brown eyes looked as serious and solemn as her mother's. Next to Trevor, she was the most adorable thing he'd ever seen and Trip was lost, just that quickly.

He patted the knee of his good leg, motioning her closer. "Yes he is. And you're such a big girl. How old are you?"

She came over and leaned on his knee, holding up three pudgy fingers. She added a fourth, then frowned, then pulled it back down.

"Three and a half," her mother translated with a laugh as she sat back down and picked up her chopsticks. "Actually she'll be four in August."

"August?" He fed Trevor another spoonful of cereal. "Hey that's when Trevor's birthday is too."

Bailey tugged on his sleeve. When he smiled down at her, she spoke shyly. "I can do that. I help with Joey."

Trip glanced over at Beth, who nodded. "You know Lisa Hayes, right? She keeps Bailey while I'm at work. Her youngest is just a little older than Trevor. Lisa says Bailey's really good with the littler ones."

Trip thought a moment, then nodded. "Okay, Bailey. Why don't you sit up here..." He pulled her onto his knee. "And give it a go." He handed her the plastic baby spoon shaped like an airplane.

She tucked her lower lip between her teeth in concentration and gripped the spoon as if it were fragile. Then she very carefully scooped up a precise amount of cereal and brought it up to Trevor's mouth.

"Here comes the airplane. Voooom."

Trip had to snicker at how eagerly Trevor slurped up the food, almost pulling the spoon from Bailey's hand. Bailey wrinkled her nose. "I guess he's hungry."

"He usually is," Trip agreed. Getting Trevor to eat had never been a problem.

Bailey repeated the process with a spoonful of applesauce from the other side of the divided dish. Back and forth, neat and tidy, until the food was gone.

"I'm impressed," Trip told her when he lifted her down from his knee. "You're even better at that than I am. He hardly made any mess at all." He gravely offered his hand. "Thank you. You were a big help. Now how about that movie?"

"Okay." She skipped over toward the big screen TV and sat down on the floor. Trip followed at a slower, uneven pace. He set Trevor in his bouncy chair and started the DVD, then returned to the table to finish his own meal.

"You've definitely got the touch," Beth told him when he sat down. "You won't believe this, but she's usually very shy with strangers."

Trip grinned. "And I'll admit to being stranger than most. She's a good kid. Reminds me a lot of her mom." He started scooping up food from his interrupted feast.

It was good to hear Beth laugh. Judging by the worry lines that bracketed her mouth, she hadn't been doing much of that lately. So while they ate he regaled her with stories from his Hollywood days.

"And I swear, she actually picked up a whole bowl of

pasta salad from the craft services table and dumped it over his head right there on the set." He finished the story of a knock-down drag-out brawl between a famous acting couple. "So he took a bottle of sparkling water, shook it up, and sprayed it right in her face."

"Oh my goodness!" She laughed until she had to pick up her napkin and wipe away a tear. "And everyone thinks they're this perfect pair!"

He cocked his head for a second. "Actually, they're better than most in that business. After the fight they spent three hours in her trailer making up. And I never once saw either of them making eyes at anyone else. So maybe, for them, it works."

"Maybe."

She offered to clean off the table while Trip fetched his laptop. Then she made him pull up a couple of websites she'd worked on, like the one for Shayna's beauty shop and one for a local tavern. Finally she asked him to show her a few other author sites that he liked.

"Okay so you need a biography page, links to your publisher, and excerpts from the novel. Do you have a recent photo I can use?"

"Yeah. They're putting my last headshot in the back of the book, so I figure we can use the same one on the site. I can email you that and my official bio."

"Sounds good." She handed him a business card with her email address.

About an hour later, Trip shut down his laptop while Beth packed up her samples and worksheets. They looked over at the television only to realize that both children were sound asleep—Trevor in his bouncer, and Bailey on the floor with a throw pillow from the sofa under her head.

They stood side by side. Beth chuckled. "They look so peaceful like that don't they?"

Trip grinned. "Yep. Almost enough to make you forget about the screaming tantrums and sleepless nights, isn't it?"

"Bailey doesn't do those often, but she does have her moments. I've got to admit though, that carrying her to the car was easier a couple of years ago." Beth leaned down and reached for her daughter, but Trip stayed her hand.

"Let me."

"Your leg..." Beth hesitated. Trip shook his head.

"It's fine. I told you, yesterday was the exception, not the norm. Don't worry, I won't drop her." He bent and carefully lifted the child into his arms. Bailey stirred slightly then wrapped her arms around his neck and snuggled up to his chest as trustingly as any of his nieces or nephews.

"In that case, be my guest." Beth led the way to the door and held it open for him so he didn't have to disturb the sleeping beauty in his arms. "I'll have all the fun of getting her up the stairs at the other end."

"You know, you never mentioned where you're living these days." He followed her out into the balmy late spring evening. "Are you in town?"

"Upstairs apartment in one of the old houses downtown," she replied. "Not far from your brother."

"Nice." Fitz and Ree had moved into a spacious old painted lady Victorian. While Trip liked his house up here on the mountain, he knew being right in the heart of town was nice for some people.

Beth sighed and opened the back door of her battered station wagon. "It's cheap."

Ah. Money problems. He'd noticed her outdated clothes and tattered briefcase. And then she'd paid for his dinner. Trip had enough sense of self-preservation not to offer to pick up the tab, but he was damn sure going to find some way to make it up to her.

He settled Bailey into her car seat. The model was similar enough to Trevor's that he managed the straps easily. No skimping here, he noticed. He was glad Bailey's safety rated top of the line.

"So, I'll draw up some preliminary designs," Beth said as she checked her daughter, then smiled when Trip held open the driver's door for her. "Would next week be okay to get back with you?"

"Sounds good. Only this time it will be my turn to treat for dinner. You can just pick Bailey up and meet me—here or at your house, whichever is more convenient."

"Oh!"

He didn't know why she sounded so startled by the idea. She'd been up here now two nights in a row.

She fastened her seat belt. "Here, I guess. Six o'clock?"

"Next Thursday at six it is." He fought the urge to lean over and give her a kiss before he closed the door, but decided that would probably scare her out of coming back. "Drive safe."

He watched as she pulled down the drive until she rounded the first curve, then made his way back inside. Trevor was still zonked out in his chair, so Trip grabbed his laptop and sat down in his recliner. The end of the video was still playing for background noise as he began to type.

What had he been thinking of, to almost kiss Beth? He hadn't even dated in the year since his accident, the last thing he needed to do was jump into something with an old friend, someone who wouldn't just wave and walk away before things got serious. He was so swamped right now with Trevor and his new career that there was no room in his life for a woman—especially one that came with an all too serious three-and-a-half-year-old girl.

Chapter Three

She wasn't supposed to be excited about seeing him. It was just a business meeting, Beth told herself over and over Wednesday evening as she laid out her clothes for the next day.

She'd spent all week reminding herself of the reasons why she needed to steer clear of Trip Hall. He was everything she couldn't afford in her life—handsome, charming, reckless, and feckless. He'd just about gotten himself killed for a movie for goodness sake! If she ever did get involved with another man in this lifetime it was going to be someone nice and stable and safe. Someone who thought about things like investing and insurance and retirement—and fidelity.

The phone rang, startling her out of her funk. Who the heck could it be at this hour of the night? Was something wrong with Shayna or one of her kids?

"Hello?"

There was no response. No voice at all on the other end.

"Hello?"

Still nothing. Must be the current favorite prank of some local teenager. That was the third call like that she'd gotten this week. Shaking her head, she switched off the phone and went back to stare at her closet.

She pulled out a dove gray pantsuit and a pale blue blouse—one that buttoned nice and high at the neckline. She needed to make sure Trip knew their friendship was that and nothing more—an old acquaintanceship now morphing into a client-consultant relationship.

None of which did anything to explain why butterflies were line dancing in her stomach the next day as she made her way up the drive to his cabin.

The wooden front door was open when she arrived and the warm spicy aroma of Italian food wafted out to her through the screen.

"Anybody home?" In Shirley, if the door was open it was considered rude to knock or ring the doorbell.

"Come on in," Trip called out to her. "The sauce is almost ready."

She held the door for Bailey. This time she'd known they were coming up here, so Bailey carried a backpack with some coloring books and toys. Beth had her briefcase with the designs for Trip's website.

The table was set for three, with Trevor's high chair in the fourth spot. The toddler was happily munching and playing with a pile of Cheerios as his father moved about the kitchen, tossing a salad and stirring a big sauce pan on the stove.

"Well, if it isn't the two prettiest ladies in Shirley." He gave Beth and Bailey a blinding smile. He wore jeans and a pale pink polo shirt which made Beth smile back. She doubted there was another man in town secure enough in his masculinity to wear a pink shirt with absolutely no self-consciousness whatsoever. Her smile dropped as she realized it was just another sign of what she already knew. Even though he'd said he was here to stay, Shirley wasn't likely to hold Trip for long. Pretty soon he'd go back to craving the bright lights of Los Angeles, and forget all about the people and places he left behind.

"I didn't know you could cook," she teased as she got Bailey settled at the coffee table with her coloring book to wait until dinner was ready.

"Well, I like to eat," he returned. "So learning to cook seemed like a smart thing to do at the time."

"I thought everyone ate out all the time in Hollywood."

He gave a little snort of laughter, then transferred the aromatic sauce to a white china bowl that looked like it had probably been his grandmother's. "Don't believe everything you read. Sure there are plenty of people out there who do live that insane lifestyle, but there are plenty of others who don't. Unless you're one of the big names, you can't afford it anyway. Most of the people who *work* in show business are pretty ordinary people."

She returned to the kitchen. "Anything I can do to

help?"

"Hand me that colander, would you?"

She handed him the oversized copper strainer from the counter. He set the strainer in the sink before dumping the big pot of pasta into it to drain. She eyed the mound with skepticism. "Isn't that an awful lot of food for just the three of us?"

He turned to her with a grin. "I didn't say I liked cooking every day. This will taste even better for lunch tomorrow—and maybe the next day."

Without asking, she transferred the bowls of sauce and salad to the table, while Trip removed a warm loaf of bread from the oven and laid it on a cutting board to slice.

"There's salad dressing and butter in the fridge," he said over his shoulder. "And the iced tea, or lemonade if you prefer. I like a half and half mix if you want to pour."

She laughed as she walked to the fridge. "You always did like weird combinations. I remember the choco-vanilla-rootbeer-orange float you talked Ruthanne into making you one summer. Ick!"

"Yeah. Being a self-respecting teenage boy I would never admit it at the time, but that one was pretty nasty." He finished transferring food to the table just as she poured herself a glass of lemonade, and a glass of milk for Bailey.

"I think we're all set." He handed Trevor a sippy cup off the counter while Beth got Bailey situated. "Trevor already had his dinner, this is just his dessert. If we're lucky, we'll get through our meal before he gets bored sitting here."

Before Beth could sit, Trip had pulled out the chair next to Bailey's. She almost stumbled at the unexpected courtesy, but she managed to pull herself out of it in time to accept and nod at him politely. "Thank you."

He gave her a teasing bow. "Just because I moved to California for a few years doesn't mean I forgot everything my parents and grandparents drilled into my head for the first eighteen years. I'm thick, but not stupid."

"No." She unfolded her napkin into her lap, helped Bailey do the same. "I know better. You were never thick. Just a bit unmotivated when it came to academics."

He laughed. "Which is a very polite way of saying

lazy."

"You said it. I didn't."

They started to eat and the casual banter continued, which was no surprise. They fell back into the comfortable camaraderie of old friends. What continued to impress Beth was how easily he included Bailey. Most grown ups tended to ignore anyone under eighteen sitting at the table. But not Trip. Given his number of nieces and nephews, she guessed it shouldn't have, but somehow it still struck her as odd when Trip asked the little girl what she liked to do in the summertime.

"I like playing outside with Miss Lisa's dog," she answered seriously. "And swimming."

"Lisa has an inflatable kiddy pool they use," Beth explained.

Trip kept his eyes on Bailey. "Really? I have a pond that your mom and I used to swim in when we were younger. Maybe this summer you and your mom can come out and see if it still works."

She nibbled on her lip in thought, then looked up at Beth, eyes wide with hope. "I've never gone in a pond. But if Mommy's there it might be okay."

Beth had been about to refuse, but the longing in Bailey's gaze won out. "We'll see. Maybe some Saturday we could visit." She cocked her head at Trip. "You've maintained the pond? Even when you weren't living here?" That struck her as a colossal waste of his money and somebody's time. Keeping it clean and free of weeds enough for swimming couldn't be an easy task.

"Harper's kids like to use it," he explained. "Their spread is on this end of the county, so it's just a few minutes in the car to bring the kids over, and she has the keys. They kept an eye on the place for me while I was out of state."

"Oh." Of course. His sister and brother-in-law had probably maintained the pond in return for its use. Once again she found herself envying his close-knit family. One of her biggest regrets was that, like her mom, Bailey was doomed to be an only child all her life.

Trevor started to fuss, and Trip excused himself briefly to change his son and deposit him in his play pen in the living room while they finished their meal. Once he returned, they kept the talk light, and Beth breathed a mental sigh of relief. They were back to being friends, apparently. Trip seemed to have gotten past his need to flirt and charm like he did with every female he met. At least she told herself she was relieved, not hurt like she'd been in high school. Back then she'd wanted so desperately for him to look at her the way he did the more glamorous girls.

"Do you want some more milk, Bailey?"

Lost in her thoughts, Beth hadn't noticed her daughter's empty glass, but Trip had.

"Yes please." Bailey picked up her small juice glass to hand it to Trip as he stood and walked to the fridge. As her daughter turned to watch Trip move, she slipped off her chair and tumbled to the floor. The glass shattered and Bailey began to cry.

Beth leaped up out of her chair, but Trip was closer. He scooped the little girl up in his arms and plopped her bottom down on the counter. He kept one big hand on her shoulder to hold her in place while he caught her little fists in his other.

"Let me see your hands, Bailey. Did you cut yourself?"

"I-I'm s-s-s-or-rr-ry," Bailey stuttered.

Moving in close to Trip, Beth caught her daughter's hand. "Open," she instructed.

Bailey uncurled one palm into Beth's hand, but her eyes were brimming over and gazing up at Trip.

"It's okay, kiddo. It's just a glass. Accidents happen." His voice was so soothing even Beth felt some of the tension ease from her spine. "We just want to make sure you didn't get hurt. Now open your fingers for me, okay?"

With a trust that she'd never shown another stranger, Bailey unfolded the fingers of her other hand into Trip's. Beth watched him carefully inspect the tiny digits while he made goofy faces at Bailey to distract her. "Nope, no damage here. How about on your side, Mom?"

Beth hurriedly checked Bailey's other hand, trying to ignore the flip her stomach did when Trip placed a loud smacking kiss on the hand he held. "Nope. All clean." She matched the kiss on Bailey's other hand. Then she kissed her daughter on the nose. "You can stop crying, sweetie.

No boo-boos today."

"Tell you what." Trip made another funny face at Bailey, earning him a tentative grin through the sheen of tears. "I'll clean up the mess, but first you have to give me a hug. Do we have a deal?"

Beth's heart stuttered for a second before he realized he was talking to her daughter and not her. Bailey sniffled and nodded, then threw her chubby little arms around Trip's neck and squeezed. She watched as the big man gently returned the embrace and smiled.

"That was a really good hug. Now you two stay right where you are so nobody steps on any glass."

He snagged a dishtowel off a hook beside the sink and used it to pick up the biggest pieces of the glass, then shook it out into the trash can. Beth tried very hard to ignore the smooth ripple of the muscles beneath his knit shirt as he then reached into the pantry for a broom and dustpan, swiftly dispensing with the rest of the mess. At least now that he wasn't standing so close she was no longer breathing in his war, slightly spicy scent. She lifted Bailey into her arms and held her close, trying to get her heart rate back down to normal.

Trip ushered them all back into their seats and gave them one of his heart-stopping grins. "Okay. Now who wants dessert?"

****

Trip wasn't sure how he managed to get through the entire meal without flirting openly with Beth. Something about her supercharged all the hormones that he'd thought were more or less dormant since his accident. After dinner was through, Bailey settled down to watch another cartoon while Beth laid out her design ideas for Trip's website.

"These are good," he mused, scrolling down the screen on her laptop. He couldn't help but notice it was an old one, though she'd obviously splurged on the necessary software for her fledgling business. "I like the colors and the layout. But I'm curious. Why the cowboy hat in the logo? The book's about a stuntman, not a cowboy."

She gave him one of those looks women reserve for men when they're being particularly thick. "It's *your* website, silly. It's not just for the one book. The cowboy hat is an indicator of you."

"But I'm not a cowboy. I might have been raised on a ranch, but it's been a long time since I competed in junior rodeos. I sure as heck can't rope or herd at the moment." He pointed down at his gimpy leg.

She rolled her eyes again. "Once a cowboy, always a cowboy, buster."

Hmm. Why did it sound like she meant something else entirely? Somewhere along the way his buddy Lizzie had grown up into a woman as enigmatic as any other.

And that thought brought up another question he'd been dying to ask. "Why'd you change your name?"

Her face shuttered instantly, all the humor and camaraderie vanishing in an instant. "I just—wanted to start over I guess. Build a new life for myself after my husband died."

All his instincts told him she was telling the truth, but only part of it. Had she loved her late husband so much that she couldn't bear to hear the name he used to call her? He felt like an absolute bastard for envying a dead man. "It suits you," he managed. "The new hair style, the contacts..." He was guessing on those, but she wasn't wearing glasses any more. "The name Beth—it's sweet, ladylike. It suits you."

Jeez, could he sound any more pathetic? It helped that she didn't seem to think so. Instead her skin turned a pretty shade of pink and she smiled.

"Thanks. You know Rick Anderson's the local optometrist now, right? He's married to Shayna. They gave me a year's supply of contacts for Christmas. And she gives me a big discount on hair cuts."

"I'm sure she's glad to have you back in town."

Beth and Shayna though opposite in many ways had always been best friends in high school. Trip hadn't seen too much of the hairdresser since he'd been back, but she'd made a point to stop in and say hi when he was covering for Ree at the bookstore. She'd even invited him to come to dinner some time. He'd been buddies with her husband Rick all through school too. Maybe he should tell her he'd come if she invited Beth and Bailey as well. Though that could open him up to all kinds of speculation he'd probably rather avoid. He forced his attention back to the web site.

Once he'd approved the designs and suggested very few changes, they argued about her rates. For some reason, she tried to give him a steep discount, and he wrote the check out for the price Ree had told him was normal. After she grudgingly accepted it, they finished their coffee in companionable silence.

Bailey and Trevor were both sacked out in the living room, so there was no rush for Beth to leave, but there was also no real reason for her to stay. Since he now had no further excuse to bring her out here, though, Trip was reluctant to let her go. He knew he should just back away, go back to being the kind of friend who smiled and said hello if he ran into her in town, but he didn't want that. Something about being around Beth—and her daughter—soothed an achy spot in his soul that he hadn't even known was bruised. Even though she stirred up parts of him he wished she didn't, it was worth it just to be near her, to get to talk to her. He hadn't known how much he'd missed her friendship, her keen wit and goofy sense of humor over the last fourteen years.

Beth drained her mug then stood and stretched. "Well, tomorrow is a work day, so I'd better get going. Thanks for dinner. And the business." She held out a hand to shake as Trip pulled himself upright.

"Hey, you're the best. Who else would I want designing and maintaining my portal to the world? Thanks for doing it." Then he did what he'd wanted to do since he'd seen her in the park. He took hold of her outstretched hand and tugged her close, wrapping her in a bear hug she couldn't escape. After a second of hesitation, she went with it. She wrapped her arms around his waist and squeezed, but she kept her head down, burrowed into his chest. No way was he getting a kiss out of this he decided. But a hug was a start.

She wasn't short, but she wasn't particularly tall either, and the top of her head tucked comfortably right beneath his chin. He tipped his nose down to inhale the soft strawberry fragrance of her hair. Then he stepped back before she could feel the way his body was responding to her closeness. All her signals still said she wasn't looking for a relationship, and he didn't want to scare her away.

"See you again soon," he told her as she gathered up her things. This time he didn't even ask, he just scooped Bailey up without waking her and carried her out to the car.

"Of course," she replied.

He thought she was trying for breezy, but she didn't quite make it. Good. He wanted her to be as affected by the chemistry between them as he was.

"Shirley's not that big a town. We're bound to run into each other."

That wasn't what he'd meant, and he was pretty sure she knew it. He kissed the top of Bailey's head as he strapped her into her car seat, then turned to find that Beth had already gotten in. She moved to close her door, but he stayed it with his hand.

"Drive safe," he told her. He took the seat belt from her hand and fastened it around her much like he'd just done for her daughter. "I'll give you a call this weekend, if that's okay."

He could see her start to form the word, "Why," but she apparently thought the better of it and nodded instead. "Fine."

Unable to resist, he leaned down and kissed the top of her head too. She smelled as sweet as her daughter, but in a very, very different way. "Goodnight."

Then he stepped back and watched as she drove away.

He whistled as he went back inside.

****

What was she going to do about him?

Beth got Bailey into bed, then decided she'd earned a long hot bubble bath. One of the few amenities her apartment offered was a big old claw foot tub in the bathroom. She poured a dollop of bubble-gum scented goop into the tub, thinking that one of these days she had to splurge on some grown-up bath products. Maybe she'd use a little of the money Trip had paid her for a few personal luxuries, the kind she'd given up on since Daniel's death—heck, even before.

The phone rang just as she climbed into the tub, and while every instinct she possessed urged her to jump out and answer it, she managed to talk herself into remaining in the suds. *That's why they invented answering machines.* Besides, it was probably just her prank caller again. She told herself those weren't worth getting annoyed about. Whoever it was would get tired of the game soon enough.

She leaned back against the edge of the tub and closed her eyes.

What was she going to do about Trip? She couldn't believe he'd actually kissed her. Surely it had been an impulse but it had still left her pulse pounding and her heart racing.

He was handsome, fun, daring and charming—everything she didn't need in a man. Even if she had been willing to consider letting another man into her life, she couldn't, not for her own sake or Bailey's, let it be another attractive ne'er-do-well. *You'd think you'd have learned that lesson by now, Elizabeth Ann. The pretty ones always let you down in the end.* She'd let Trip Hall into her life once before, and look how well that had turned out. She'd slunk off to college with a broken heart.

Not for the first time, she thought about the similarities between Trip and her late husband Daniel. Had she fallen for Daniel because he reminded her so much of Trip? Both had thick dark hair and blue eyes, not to mention a great body, a slick style and oodles of charm.

But there were differences too, and she was almost afraid to admit that. She'd convinced herself over the years that the two men were exactly the same, but Daniel would never have carried Bailey to the car, let alone kissed the little girl goodnight, or been so concerned and patient over the broken glass. He'd died when Bailey was just a couple months old, but even then he'd had no tolerance for the crying and mess that went hand in hand with babies. She didn't remember him changing one diaper or getting up once in the night to check on Bailey. He'd have never been the doting, devoted single father she'd seen when she'd watched Trip with his son.

But being a good father and being a good husband were far from the same thing. She had to remind herself that her responsibility as a mother far outweighed any lustful thoughts she might be feeling as a woman. Even if

Trip was in enough of a slump to consider giving someone as drab as she a whirl, there was no way it could be anything but a fling. And a fling wasn't something she could afford to indulge in. The last thing she was willing to see happen was for Bailey to get attached to a father figure who wouldn't stick around. If Beth ever did get involved with another man, it had to be someone stable and secure—someone who wouldn't cheat and run around and put his own desires ahead of his responsibilities.

Bailey would never remember the father who had died when she was less than a year old, and as much as Beth hated to admit it, that was in many ways a blessing. There had been no evil in Daniel. He'd never raised a hand to either of them, but his idea of affection had been to bellow "I love you," at the top of his lungs after coming home drunk. By the time Bailey was born he didn't even do that. As soon as Beth had started gaining weight with her pregnancy, Daniel had been through with her. He had no use for a fat wife, not when there were plenty of skinny young things to be found at the local tavern.

He'd also never understood the concept of responsibility. Jobs were boring or confining or stupid, and he never lasted at one more than a few months. Beth had managed to keep them mostly afloat on the wages from her accounting position, but it had always been tight, and Daniel had always frittered away every penny he could get his hands on. After he'd died, Beth had discovered that he'd owed an enormous amount of money. He'd taken several credit cards without her knowledge and run every one of them up to the limit. Their condo was on the verge of repossession. Three years later, she was just starting to emerge from under the mountain of debt.

Trip has a job, whispered an annoying voice in her brain. She shook her head. *Sort of*. Though having read his book, she was more inclined to take his new career seriously. He was as good at writing as he'd always been at everything else. Rhiannon had groused that he wouldn't let her pay him for his work in the shop during her honeymoon. So he wasn't sponging off his family. He accepted their help when he needed it, but he gave back when he could. Try as she might, she couldn't find any irresponsibility in that.

If only he hadn't crushed her dreams back in high school. She wasn't sure she could ever forgive him for prom night. Neither of them had had a date, so he'd agreed to pick her up. In her mind, though, it had been a date. Until she'd caught him kissing Pam Davenport behind the stack of speakers in the corner.

But that had been years ago and had no bearing on the adults either of them had grown up to be.

The bathwater had grown cold while Beth lay there thinking about Trip. The chill brought her out of her funk and she pulled the rubber plug with her toes and stood, then reached for a towel. She looked at it and grinned. Maybe one day she'd even splurge on towels that weren't printed with cartoon princesses. For now, she'd make do. Being Bailey's mom was more rewarding than anything else anyway.

****

Being the youngest in a big family had taught Trip plenty about being sneaky. With four older siblings watching his every move, he'd learned early on to plan carefully when he really wanted to get away with something. So now he put those skills to work, trying to figure out how to spend more time with Beth.

Shayna was a possible ally, as was his sister-in-law Ree. But letting either of them in on his machinations meant letting the whole Hall clan, if not the whole damn town in on them. Trip wasn't ready for that yet.

He couldn't even quite figure out why it was so all-fired important. Sure, Beth was an old friend, but he was fast coming to the realization that his motives went beyond renewing the old acquaintance. He and Lizzie had been teenage buddies. His feelings for Beth were those of a man for an attractive and appealing woman.

Wasn't that just a kick in the ass?

Getting involved with a woman had been nowhere in his game plan for the near future. Sure, he'd thought about finding a wife like his brothers had some day. After his leg was healed and Trevor was older and his new career was off and running. Not now when he could barely walk on a bad day and still used a cane on a good one. Besides, his experience with Lorelei had taught him he wasn't exactly smart when it came to picking women, so he had planned to avoid entanglements altogether, at least for a while.

But he couldn't get Beth out of his mind. He went to sleep thinking about silky blonde hair and big brown eyes, then woke up hard as a rock. And Bailey—damn if that little thing hadn't stolen his heart the moment he'd met her. It was too late to try to convince himself he just wanted to be friends with either of them. No, Trip was man enough to admit he was a goner. Now he just had to figure out what to do about it.

Chapter Four

It took him a week and the help of the local Veterans of Foreign Wars post to figure out his next move.

He was leaning on the counter in the bookstore chatting with Ree when one of the Auxiliary members came in selling tickets to the carnival they were hosting to raise money for their scholarship fund. As a concerned citizen and a veteran himself, he couldn't buy just one, could he? Trevor certainly didn't need his own, and Trip checked to be sure that Bailey was under the age requirement as well.

"Okay, spill it," Ree demanded after she'd purchased tickets for her and Fitz and sent the elderly lady on her way with a homemade cookie.She plopped onto her stool behind the counter. Trip checked on Trevor who was still napping in his stroller then leaned his elbows on the glass topped counter across from her.

"Come on, Trip. What's going on in that twisty little brain of yours?"

"What? Just being a good neighbor," he insisted.

"Yeah and I'm Mary Queen of Scots. You're up to something."

"Well, I hear she may have been a redhead."

Ree laughed. "Okay, I'll back off. Just—be careful, all right? I know you've had a pretty crappy time in the last year or so, and I worry about you sometimes."

Didn't everybody? But Trip knew his big-hearted sister-in-law really meant what she said. He shook his head. "Don't. You just worry about yourself. And that niece or nephew you're going to be giving me soon."

Ree's big green eyes flew open. "Fitz told you?"

Trip chuckled softly. "No. But the saltines you tried to hide behind the cash register were a dead giveaway. Everything going all right?"

Her grin was as big as a mountain. She had the glow,

all right."Perfect."

"You need any help here at the shop, you call me, all right? No lifting boxes of books or rearranging the furniture on your own."

"Promise." She traced an x over her chest with her finger. "As long as you let me practice once in a while by babysitting the munchkin over there."

"Deal." His brother was one lucky bastard.

Trip couldn't help but envy his brother the chance to go through all the stages with the woman he loved. He'd missed out on that with Trevor—the pregnancy, the birth, the first few weeks. Most especially he'd missed out on the 'woman he loved' part. It had never been that way between him and Lorelei. Their relationship had been superficial at best—he'd never really seen a future in it, though he'd have stood by her had he been able to stand—and had he known about the baby. Truth be told, he was surprised she'd gone through with the pregnancy at all. Grateful to his bones, but surprised. Then she'd gotten herself killed before he could ask for an explanation.

"So, Sunday dinner at the ranch, right?" Ree's words pierced his fog of contemplation.

"Umm—yeah, of course." CJ and Allie tried to get them all together once a month or so, and despite his grumbling, Trip enjoyed the chance to spend time with his siblings.

"That's when we were going to make the big announcement." She wrinkled her cute little nose at him. "But somebody had to go and figure it out ahead of time."

"Don't worry, I know how to keep my mouth shut. I won't spoil the moment by telling anyone."

"Maybe if things go well with whoever you bought that ticket for on Saturday, you could bring her out to the ranch with you on Sunday."

Trip chuckled. "And subject both of us to the third degree? Somehow I don't think so. Even if she does agree to go to the carnival with me, we're nowhere near the bringing her to a family dinner stage."

Ree's gaze narrowed. "But you thought about it. Just for a second. This is serious, isn't it?"

Trip shrugged. "To be honest, I have no idea."

"But you think it could be."

On his part, maybe. He turned his head away with another shrug, then felt a soft hand on his shoulder.

"No pressure, bud. But if she lives in Shirley, everybody's going to find out sooner or later. I may be new to this small town stuff, but I've figured that much out."

"Uh-huh."

"Well, anyway, we're all set for the book launch party next month." Her voice had switched over to deliberately cheerful. "I think half the town is planning to show up. You're quite the hometown celebrity."

He grimaced. "Yee. Haw."

She reached out and patted him on the cheek. "Suck it up, big boy. You keep picking high-profile careers, you can't expect to avoid the spotlight all the time. Besides, everyone in town's going to buy a copy of the book. That's the whole idea, isn't it?"

She was right, of course, and he was man enough to admit it. "Umm-hmm. Write books. Sell books. Buy diapers. Pay for college in seventeen years or so. That's the plan."

"And maybe find someone to keep you company along the way."

"If that's what's in the cards, I wouldn't complain."

"Cards, schmards." She shook her finger at him. "You want it? Go get it. Start by asking this mysterious someone to the carnival on Saturday."

"Yes, ma'am."

****

"You want me to do what?" Beth couldn't believe Trip had waylaid her outside her office just to invite her to a carnival of all things. He stood there outside the back door to Mitchell's offices while Trevor gurgled cheerfully in his stroller.

"Mrs. Fergusson conned me into buying two adult tickets. Somebody ought to use the second one. And Bailey will get a kick out of it, even if she is too little for some of the rides."

"But your family…"

"Already bought their own. I checked. Even Harper's kids are already set."

"I really don't have time…"

"Come on, Beth. You have to take a break from

working once in a while. Think how much fun it will be to feed Bailey cotton candy and take her on the carousel."

The rat knew exactly how to get around her, drat him. She had been thinking of taking Bailey for that exact reason, though her frugal soul had protested the expense. Bailey would have a blast, and Beth knew Trip would go out of his way to make sure the little girl enjoyed every minute. But she wasn't sure that a carnival was a good place for a man with an injured leg. And then there was the fact that spending a whole day with Trip was as dangerous as sitting on a shoebox full of rattlesnakes.

"It's for a good cause and everything," he coaxed, turning on his blue-eyed charm. "Please?"

She'd never been able to resist that pitiful little-boy pout, not when it was coupled with the wicked twinkle in his eyes. She couldn't count how many times he'd led her into trouble with that innocent expression. Why should now be any different? She let her shoulders droop in defeat. "Fine. We'll meet you at the fairgrounds at noon."

"Uh-uh." He shook his head with slow deliberation. "I'll pick you up. That way we won't have to try and find one another in the crowd."

Oh, like she'd miss him, even if the entire population of the state showed up. Trip Hall would stand out in any herd. But she knew him, knew his stubborn pride. He wasn't going to budge on this, so she might as well give in now. "Fine."

Trip's grin was ear to ear, like she'd just done him a huge favor. "Great. I hear there's a water slide, so don't forget your swimsuit."

Swimsuit? "Don't press your luck, pal. Carnivals are fun, but there's no way you're getting me to appear in public in a bathing suit." Could you say cellulite? After all his tucked and toned Hollywood beauties, she'd bet Trip had forgotten what real thighs looked like. Especially pasty white ones like hers.

"Spoilsport." But his smile was warm and teasing, not sarcastic as she'd feared. "Bet you still love elephant ears, though."

Beth groaned. "My mouth does, my butt not so much."

"Yeah right," he said with a snort. "Like that's a

problem. You probably weigh less than this stroller."

Beth's stomach did a weird little flip at the idea that he'd noticed her figure. Then she realized it was just one of his lines like any other. "Then your stroller must have wide hips and chunky thighs too." Before he could carry this idiocy any further, she held up one hand. "I've got to go pick up Bailey before five-thirty. We'll see you Saturday, all right?"

She saw him open his mouth like he was about to say something, then stop. He nodded. "Saturday at noon, it is."

He waited until she started moving, then kept pace, pushing the stroller ahead of him. Apparently he intended to walk her to her car. In that case she had a surprise in store. She walked beside him and watched out of the corner of her eye. His limp was better today, she noticed. The creases around his eyes were shallower too. Maybe walking around all day at a carnival wouldn't be too much for him at this stage of his recovery.

They smiled and said hello to a few shoppers as they passed Ree's bookstore and the beauty shop. Trip smiled and nodded to Len Elliot at the hardware store, who simply glowered in response. Beth hoped he wasn't still angry that she'd refused to go out with him last week.

"You're not in the municipal lot?" Trip asked as they walked by the small public parking area. She saw his silver SUV sitting amid the dusty pick-ups and mini-vans. It wasn't in a handicapped space and the temporary tag wasn't hanging from the mirror. Good, he really was improving. She paused long enough be sure he intended to follow her the rest of the way, not stop here at his own vehicle. When he tipped his head, they resumed walking.

"I walk to work," she explained. "It's only four blocks, and that way I don't have to buy a city permit."

"Makes sense. Fitz and Ree both do the same. But they don't have to worry about day care—not yet anyway. Where does the sitter live?"

"A couple miles away on Pine Street. I drive Bailey out in the morning, but it's still easier to park in my own driveway and walk in to the office."

She could tell he recognized her car in the driveway. "So now you know where to pick us up on Saturday." She hoped he didn't notice how shabby and run-down the exterior was. Her landlord had inherited the property, but didn't live in Shirley, so he didn't bother to take care of it. It had gotten even worse since the lower apartment had been vacant.

"I guess I do."

She never locked her car here in Shirley. Nobody did. She wasn't surprised when Trip rolled the stroller onto the front lawn, set the brake, and then moved to open the driver's door before she could reach it. He'd always been a gentleman, even when he was kissing other girls. The reminder of prom night helped her rebuild her defenses, and she looked up at him with a polite smile as she got into the car. "See you Saturday, then."

"Uh huh." He leaned over her as she buckled her seat belt and gave her one of his wicked grins. He didn't quite get close enough to kiss her this time, thank goodness, but she could feel the warmth of him and smell the coffee on his breath. "I'm lookin' forward to it, darlin'."

It had to be her imagination, but she swore she could feel the heat of his gaze following her as she backed the station wagon out of the driveway and headed down the street. What was really odd was that Trip had nothing to do with the nagging itch at the base of her spine. It was almost as if someone else was watching her too. Someone who wasn't nearly as friendly.

****

"Stay away from him." The voice was low and sounded like someone had attempted to disguise his tone. About all she could tell was that it was too deep to have been a woman.

Beth shrieked and dropped the phone. This was the first time her mysterious caller had said anything. Now it felt personal and not like a prank.

Gingerly, she picked up the receiver and replaced it on the cradle, ignoring the harsh sounds she heard coming from the other end of the line. Fortunately Bailey was a sound sleeper, so Beth's yelp hadn't woken her up.

Should she call the sheriff? No. She didn't want to talk to the dispatcher and have the entire town laughing at her for being a scaredy-cat. Tomorrow she'd go talk to Ree, she decided. Ree would pass it along to Fitz in a confidential manner, she was sure.

Hours later she lay huddled under her quilt with the bedroom light on. *Stay away from him.* The caller had to be referring to her walking home with Trip—that's the only man she'd so much as spoken to today aside from Mitchell. But why would someone care what she did? It didn't make any sense. It's not as if anyone was interested in her. Except for Trip, and she knew that to him she was just a way to pass the time.

Who would want to target her? Had Daniel owed someone else money? Someone who couldn't claim it through legal channels and opted for terror tactics instead? Or was it someone connected to Trip? Maybe some woman wanted him and mistakenly saw Beth as some sort of threat. No, the voice had distinctly belonged to a man.

Tears leaked down her cheeks, but she brushed them away with the back of her hand. She'd gotten through the last three years; she'd get through this. She didn't have time or energy to waste on self-pity. There was always too much to do just to keep her head above water, and any spare emotional energy she possessed belonged to Bailey.

Another wave of terror washed through her as she thought about her daughter. What if whoever this was posed a threat to Bailey? That thought brought a fresh rush of tears. Unacceptable.

Okay, the first thing she had to do was call Trip. She had to cancel on the carnival for Saturday, just in case the caller had been talking about her and Trip.

She scrambled to her feet and dashed to the kitchen for her laptop. His phone number was in here somewhere. She opened up her address book software and sunk into a chair with the cordless phone. Her hands shook as she punched in his number.

"Hello?"

He'd answered quickly and didn't sound groggy. At least she hadn't woken him up.

She swallowed hard trying to steady her voice before she spoke. She must have paused a little too long, though, because he said it again, a little less patiently this time.

"It's me, Trip. It's Beth."

"Hey." Instantly the voice was soft and welcoming

again. The sheer sex appeal of it made her skin heat, despite the strain she was under. "What's up?"

"It's about S-S-Saturday," she stuttered. Damn it, why couldn't she keep the tears out of her voice? "I c-can't go w-with you."

"Beth, what's wrong?" Now there was an unfamiliar sharpness in his tone, but she knew instinctively it wasn't directed at her.

"N-nothing."

"Bullshit." Now he turned soft and coaxing. "Come on darlin'. Tell me what happened."

She bit her lower lip hard. "I—um—may have to work on Saturday." She almost got through the lie, but her voice cracked and a sob escaped.

"Beth, are you okay? Has something happened to Bailey?" The intense concern in his voice was as comforting as a warm blanket, but she knew she couldn't give into it.

"She's—she's fine. S-sleeping."

"Are you hurt? Sick?"

"N-no."

"Then what?" His voice cracked, letting her know he was truly concerned.

And then, somehow, against her better judgment, it all came spilling out.

"Okay, Beth, just sit tight, I'm on my way." She heard movement at the other end, as if he was pounding up or down the stairs. "Give me fifteen minutes. I'll get Trevor in the car and be there as soon as I can."

"No!"

"Yes." Now it was his alpha-male, not-budging-an-inch voice. "I'm hanging up now. I'll have my cell phone. If anything seems wrong, call it. Got it?"

"Okay." She didn't realize until after he hung up that he hadn't given her the number.

Moving in a fog, she started a pot of coffee and put on her bathrobe. Not five minutes later there were loud footsteps on the stairs to her apartment and a knock on her door.

"Trip?" That was silly, she told herself as fear gripped her heart. He couldn't have possibly gotten here that fast.

"Beth? It's Rhiannon," came a kind female voice from the other side of the door. "And Fitz. Trip called us. Are you all right?"

Of course he had. She clutched the neckline of her robe with one hand while the other worked the locks on the door. Once it was open, Ree Hall swept inside and enveloped Beth in a hug.

"Oh you poor thing!" Ree's red curls were tumbled and her turquoise sweatpants and purple top had obviously been hastily donned.

Fitz wore jeans and a black t-shirt, along with a tired but friendly smile. "Care to tell me what's going on?"

She gestured helplessly toward the kitchen table. "Sit, please. The coffee should be ready soon."

Ree put her arm around Beth's waist and guided her into a chair. "You sit down and talk to the sheriff. I'll take care of the coffee."

Beth nodded and as calmly as possible, she outlined the situation to Fitz. Since he was six or seven years older than her and Trip, their high school years hadn't overlapped. That made it a little easier to think of him as an authority figure than it might have been otherwise. Of course he still looked so much like Trip that she was instantly at ease. His handsome face was leaner than that of either of his brothers, though, and his eyes were dark brown instead of Trip's baby blue. Those eyes regarded her thoughtfully, hard but with no trace of judgment or recrimination.

"So tonight was the first time he's ever spoken?"

Beth nodded. "I'm sure I just overreacted. It's probably just someone's idea of a prank. But the voice sounded so…menacing, I guess I just panicked."

"Anyone would have." Ree set mugs of coffee in front of Beth and Fitz, and drew a mug full of water from the sink before sitting down in the chair next to Beth. She patted Beth's hand on top of the table.

"And his exact words were…" Fitz prodded, glancing down at the notes he was making on a pocket-sized pad.

She knew he wanted to verify her story so she repeated it. "Stay away from him."

"That's it?"

"That's all," she confirmed. "Everything I heard,

anyway. I dropped the phone. When I picked it up to hang up, he was shouting something, but I didn't listen."

"Fair enough." His smile was kind, but firm. "And what makes you think he was talking about Trip?"

Oh, crap, Trip had mentioned that part too, it seemed. She felt her face flush. "He's the only man I so much as spoke to today, besides my boss."

"Do you have any idea who it could be?"

She shook her head, then stopped and looked him in the eye. "My late husband Daniel—he owed a lot of people a lot of money. I keep thinking it could be one of his bookies or something."

"I'll see what I can find out," Fitz told her, with no trace of the disapproval she'd expected to see in his expression. "Maybe tomorrow you could make a list of any that you know about."

She nodded. "They were all in Denver, as far as I know. That's one reason I moved back here."

Just then she heard slow but heavy treads on the wooden stairs. Ree patted her hand again, then got up and moved toward the door. She was almost there when they heard a loud knock and Trip's voice bellowing, "Beth? Let me in."

"Keep your voice down," Ree scolded her brother-in-law as she opened the door. "Remember Bailey's still asleep."

"Sorry." His voice dropped to normal as he stepped inside, dropped the back-pack style diaper bag to the floor, and handed Trevor into Ree's outstretched arms. His eyes were on Beth with an intense expression that made her stomach flutter, but he took a second to drop a kiss on Trevor's head and one on Ree's cheek before he strode across the room to Beth's side and dropped into the chair Ree had vacated. He took her hand in his and studied her face. "Are you all right?"

She lifted her eyes to his with what she hoped was a smile, though she could feel it tremble. "I'm fine. Just—shaken up—I guess."

He turned his gaze on his brother refusing to let go of her hand, even when she tried to tug it away. "You think she's in any danger?"

"Doesn't look like it," Fitz told him. "At this point

there's nothing to show it's anything more than a string of crank calls."

"But?" Trip demanded, his left eyebrow lifting just a touch. Even Beth had picked up the hesitation in the sheriff's voice.

"But it feels hinky," Fitz admitted. He sighed and scrubbed one hand through his close-cropped dark hair. "And it doesn't hurt to take precautions. Call the phone company tomorrow, get your number changed to an unlisted one and get set up with Caller ID. Tell them I said to put a rush on it. Then start screening your calls."

Beth nodded, mentally calculating the additional expense. There went the new clothes she'd been thinking about for summer.

"Why don't you come home with us for the rest of the night?" Ree had taken a seat on the worn sofa across the small living room/kitchen area from the table, her nephew cuddled on her lap.

Beth shook her head. "I'm not going to let a stupid crank call chase me out of my own home," she insisted. "Besides, I don't want to wake Bailey and terrify her."

The men both nodded.

"Then I'm staying here."

Trip didn't know who was more surprised by his statement, Beth or himself. Even Fitz looked startled. Only Ree gave him a warm enigmatic smile.

He didn't know where the idea had come from, but now that it had, it wasn't budging.

"Well, then this guy is coming home with us," Ree told him, bouncing Trevor on her knee. "I'm sure there are enough supplies in the diaper bag to get him through the night. You can pick him up in the morning."

Trip felt a pang at the thought of separation, but he nodded. Though he'd rather take Beth and Bailey back to his place, he could tell she was serious about staying, and no way was he leaving her here alone. If he was going to sleep on that short, ratty couch over there, he'd sleep better knowing Trevor was safe and secure with his brother.

"Fine." Fitz drained his coffee and stood, clearly trying to stifle the smile that kept twitching at the corners of his lips. He hefted the backpack then stepped over to the couch and took Trevor from Ree's arms so she could stand. "Call if anything else comes up. Otherwise, I'm going to take these two home to bed. And don't forget to get me that list as soon as you can. I've got a friend on the force in Denver who can help me look into them."

Trip stood and limped to the door, giving his son a kiss and hug while Ree embraced Beth. "You be careful," Ree admonished. Then she turned and hugged Trip as well. "You too. The munchkin will be at the store with me in the morning, whenever you're ready to get him."

"Thanks." He looked down at his sister-in-law. Lines of fatigue crossed her pretty, elfin features, and he felt a huge pang of guilt that she'd gotten caught up in this when he'd called his brother. He'd watched his sisters go through enough pregnancies to know the first few months were exhausting. "Tell you what. I'll go open the store, and you can come in late. How's that sound?"

She laughed. "Like an offer too good to refuse. You've got a deal."

Then Fitz ushered her out the door and he was alone with Beth.

"You don't need to stay." She clutched the neckline of her ugly mud-green terry-cloth bathrobe. Pink flannel pajama bottoms patterned with cartoon bunnies peeked beneath the hem and solid pink cuffs showed at her wrists. The outfit should have been the opposite of sexy, but somehow it was the most appealing thing he'd ever seen.

"I'm not going anywhere."

"But your brother said there wasn't any danger." Her eyes stayed glued at about the level of his collarbone, refusing to look into his. Her pale skin and taut features gave her away. Whether she admitted it or not, she was scared. And damn it, so was he.

He put his finger under her chin to force her gaze upward. "My brother the sheriff said he couldn't be *sure* there was any danger. He also said it felt hinky. Which is a dumb-ass word, but his instincts are not. If the situation feels wrong to him, then it probably is."

She bit her lower lip, which was already red and puffy, probably from her chewing on it in her distress. He couldn't resist the urge to stroke the abused flesh with the pad of his thumb. Heat rocketed through his body from just that slight touch. He was in way over his head.

"I'll be fine," she insisted. She licked her lip with the tip of her tongue, just barely grazing his thumb. The sensation speared straight to his groin. "You can't stay here. There's nowhere for you to sleep."

He swallowed hard, trying to force his sudden arousal under control, and tipped his head toward the couch. "I'll manage." His voice cracked, just a little.

"But..." Her warm brown eyes lost their focus and her cheeks took on a tinge of pink. Then she bit her lip again and shrugged. "But why?"

"Do you really have to ask?"

She nodded, just a hint of a movement as he still held her chin.

Trip groaned. "Because of this."

He really hadn't intended to kiss her. Not tonight, not so soon, not like this.

But standing there toe to toe in her tiny little apartment, he simply couldn't help himself. With one hand on her chin, and the other wrapping itself around her waist to pull her close, he lowered his head and took her lips.

****

Beth knew that letting Trip kiss her was a very bad idea. So why did it have to feel so darned good?

His lips were gentle, coaxing against hers. His breath smelled of coffee and peppermint, while the rest of him smelled like warm, sweaty male. He was wearing jeans and a baggy sweatshirt. Her fingers burrowed into the soft fleece sleeves and gripped, even while she told herself she was supposed to be pushing him away.

The hand under her chin slipped around her neck and sifted through her hair as he tilted his head to change the angle of the kiss. When his tongue probed softly against the seam of her lips, she opened, welcoming him inside.

So this is what it was like to kiss Trip Hall.

It was every fantasy she'd ever had in high school, and then some.

The bulky knot of her bathrobe's belt acted as a bundling board between their bodies, preventing her from plastering herself as closely against him as she'd have liked. As his tongue explored every ridge and crevice inside her mouth, her nipples hardened and rasped against the cotton of her pajama top, and moisture dampened the flannel between her legs.

Oh, lord it had been so long. And even with Daniel she'd never gone up in flames like this, not from a simple kiss.

The kiss didn't stop until they were both out of breath. She wasn't sure if the groan she heard came from his mouth or hers as he dragged his lips away and pressed her face into the curve below his chin. He dropped another soft kiss on the top of her head and held her close.

"You going to be able to sleep?" he murmured, his breath still warm against her ear.

After *that?* Beth wasn't sure she could speak coherently yet so she just shrugged.

"It's okay, darlin'. I'm not going to let anything happen, to you or Bailey."

Oh. That's what he meant. For just a second there she'd actually forgotten about the threatening call. As soon as he mentioned it, though, all the fear came flooding back. She wrapped her arms around his waist and clung, giving in to the need for comfort. It had been so long since she'd had anyone to hold onto. She knew this wasn't real, wouldn't last, but just for tonight it was so nice to lean into his big strong body and feel safe.

Trip just stood there, holding her tight and stroking his hands up and down her back, soothing her while she trembled and fought the tears. The strong arms circling her body felt like a haven and his sweatshirt was soft and warm against her cheek. His lips grazed the top of her head.

Somewhere along the way, Trip eased them both down onto the sofa without breaking off his embrace. She sat sideways across his lap with her face still buried in his shoulder until the quivering stopped.

"Better?"

She jumped at the sound of his voice breaking the cocoon of fantasy she'd begun to spin. A beautiful fantasy where she got to spend every night wrapped in Trip's arms, surrounded by his spicy, masculine scent.

"Y-yeah," she managed.

"So what did my brother mean about a list?"

She shook her head. "Nothing."

Trip tsked and tapped her nose with a finger. "Not buying that one, sweetheart. Spill it."

She didn't want to do this, didn't want to bring Daniel's ghost into the room between them. But she knew Trip's stubborn streak all too well, knew once he got his teeth into something there was no getting him to let go.

She sighed and tried to shift off his lap, but he tightened his arms refusing to let her move.

"Uh-uh. You're not going anywhere until I hear the whole story."

"But why?"

He growled, a low rumble in his chest that she felt as much as heard. "Thought I'd just answered that question. But if that kiss wasn't enough, how about the fact that we were friends, once upon a time? Good friends. Damn it, I *care* what happens to you Beth. And I want to know who hurt you so badly that you can't bring yourself to trust a man you've known nearly all your life."

You did, she wanted to say. But that part of the conversation she really wasn't up to having tonight. Instead she leaned more heavily into his shoulder. "Fine. But remember you asked for it."

"Duly noted." He squeezed her in a warm hug, then relaxed his arms so they looped around her loosely, but he still didn't let her go.

"Daniel—my husband—liked to live the high life. And to gamble. And drinking and women and everything else. He owed a lot of people a lot of money when he died. Some legitimate, others not. I've barely managed to pay off the legitimate ones. The only reason I can think of that someone would be harassing me is if they wanted to make me suffer in return for one of Daniel's debts."

"Son of a bitch!" For just a second his fingers curled into her back, then slowly relaxed. "I mean I'm sorry for your loss, darlin', but what kind of man would get himself into that kind of trouble when he's got a wife and daughter at home to support?"

"Support?" she snorted. "You've got to be kidding. That was my responsibility. Daniel never held a job for more than a few months at a time. They held him back, he said. He always had these great big schemes for getting rich, but surprise, surprise, they never seemed to work out."

"Jackass."

He muttered it under his breath, but she was so close, she couldn't miss the epithet. Grimly she nodded against his chest.

"Even after you had Bailey?"

"Uh-huh. Fortunately the accounting firm I worked for offered paid maternity leave and health insurance. And we had a really great neighbor who looked after Bailey while I was at work."

He didn't say anything, but she could feel the waves of tension radiating from muscles gone taut.

"Trip, you have to understand, this is why I can't, won't get involved in another relationship. My ability to trust—it just isn't there anymore. And I can't risk Bailey becoming attached to someone who's going to break her heart."

"Did he hurt you?"

In so many ways. But she understood what Trip was trying to ask. "Not physically. Once I got pregnant, I don't think he so much as touched me. A fat wife wasn't his idea of a good time. By then, though, I was more relieved than anything."

"You're not still in love with him, are you?" His tone was hesitant, almost as if this question was terribly important to him.

"No. I wasn't even before he died." She shrugged and hid her face in his shirt again. "When I first got pregnant they ran a bunch of tests. I found out I had a venereal disease. And I'd never slept with anyone but Daniel in my entire life."

"The man's damn lucky he's already dead." He squeezed her tight again and rocked her back and forth. "Are you okay now? Bailey?"

She nodded. "Yeah. Fortunately it was one of the ones that clear up quickly with antibiotics. And Bailey is fine, thank God! No damage from that at all."

"Thank God!" he echoed. Silence stretched between them for a moment then he spoke again. "I had wondered if you changed your name from Lizzie to Beth because you missed your husband so much you couldn't stand to hear the name he called you."

"No." The sound that emerged from her throat was somewhere between a laugh and a sob. "Exactly the other way around. Every time someone called me Lizzie, I could hear him mocking me, calling me a boring little bean-counter, too plain to keep her man interested. When I moved back here, I wanted, needed to start over."

"Boring? Plain? He was blind then, as well as stupid. There's not a damn thing plain about you, Elizabeth Ann." He pulled her face out of his shoulder and leaned down to kiss her mouth.

He remembered her middle name. She wasn't sure why that little tidbit warmed her heart, but it did. He kept the kiss light this time, and gentle. When it was over, he drew a deep ragged breath and shifted beneath her. Even through the thick fabric of her robe and pajamas, she could feel his erection straining at his jeans, and a warm tingling thrill rippled through her. Even if it was just the heat of the moment, right now Trip Hall wanted *her*. That was maybe the biggest compliment she'd ever been given.

"And it's not like my track record is any better, you know. Lorelei never even mentioned she was pregnant when she walked out. If she hadn't died, if she hadn't put my name on the birth certificate for some strange reason, I'd have never even known Trevor existed."

"Bitch." It was her turn to be infuriated now. Trip might not be her idea of a steady, responsible husband, but there was no doubting he was an incredible father. "She didn't deserve you. Or Trevor."

She felt his ragged sigh stir the hair on the top of her head. "No, but she didn't deserve to die like that either. I'd thought she was at least smart enough not to mix drinking and driving. It's a miracle Trevor wasn't killed as well. Thank God for car seats."

Beth shifted so she could wrap her arms around Trip's neck and give him a comforting hug. "Amen. I know what you mean though. I wished Daniel out of my life a hundred times, but I never wished him dead."

"How did he die? Pneumonia is pretty treatable these

days."

"Not if you refuse to get treatment. He got in a fight on the way home from the bar one night, and ended up spending the night on the sidewalk in the pouring rain. But he hated doctors, said they were all just quacks out to take your money. I tried to make him go, but that's the one time he actually tried to hit me. So I left him, took the baby to the neighbor and went to work. When I came home that night he was unconscious, so I called an ambulance." She drew in a deep breath and let it out slowly. "It was too late. He died the next day. His body was so worn down from the alcohol, drugs, and other infections, that it just gave out, the doctor said."

"I'm so sorry you had to go through all that." His words were hoarse, as if he was forcing them past a lump in his throat. But you're smart enough to know that none of it was your fault. And that not every man is made of the same sorry material."

"I know that. I just... I just can't seem to tell, you know? I was so infatuated with Daniel in the beginning. He was handsome, charming, fun. I really believed in the image he projected. How can I trust my judgment after that? And now I have Bailey to consider. What if the next time I picked a guy who actually hit us—or worse? I can't afford to take that chance."

"If you say so."

She heard the disbelief in his words, but was relieved when he didn't push it. He just kept her cradled there in his arms for several long, glorious minutes. Finally he flexed his leg and flinched.

"Nice as this is, I think the leg is starting to object. And you've got to work in the morning. I think it's time for you to say goodnight."

"I'm sorry." She scrambled off his lap, horrified at the thought of causing him pain. "You really, really don't need to stay here."

"I've slept in worse places. I'll manage. Though I wouldn't say no to a blanket, if you've got a spare."

"Of course!" She dashed into the bedroom she shared with Bailey and pulled one of the pillows from her own bed, and the extra quilt that she kept folded across the foot. "The bathroom is right there." She pointed at the only other door off the hallway and he raised one eyebrow.

"You and Bailey share a bedroom?"

Beth nodded reluctantly. "And who knew three year old girls snore?"

Trip laughed at that, the sound warm and sweet. "Well that sure removes any temptation I might have had about sneaking into your bed in the middle of the night."

Beth gasped. Did he mean it? Was he really tempted? Butterflies started dancing in her stomach.

While she stood there flummoxed, Trip took the quilt and pillow out of her hand, dropping a quick kiss on her cheek as he leaned forward. "Goodnight, Beth."

She felt the heat as her skin flushed. "Goodnight." With that, she turned and fled into her room.

Chapter Five

Trip woke after a restless night to find himself being stared at by a pair of wide brown eyes, which were approximately six inches from the tip of his nose. It took him a second to remember where he was—which explained why he ached in a dozen different places. Beth's couch was way too short for humans. It took him another half second to recognize Bailey who was pondering him intently.

When she realized his eyes were open, she gave him a brief smile. "Hi." Her smooth pale brow was furrowed in an almost comical copy of her mother's typical perplexed expression.

"Hi, yourself." He smiled back.

"Why are you here?"

Okay he was supposed to figure out an appropriate answer to that before he'd even had a cup of coffee? To tell the truth he wasn't entirely sure himself. And the last thing he wanted to do was scare the little girl.

In the back of his mind he began his usual morning mental inventory of aches and pains. The leg was stiff, but not spasming, which was good. Lower back felt like he'd slept on a sack of hammers, but based on the condition of this couch, he may well have. He was still in his jeans and hooded sweatshirt, but he'd kicked off his boots. Assured that he was decent, he slowly sat up, taking the quilt with him, and patted the cushion his torso had just vacated.

"Is your mom awake?" He'd decided asking questions of his own was the best way to avoid answering hers.

Bailey climbed up next to him and shook her head. "She won't wake up till the buzzer goes off. I'm allowed to come out here and play until she gets up, but I have to be quiet."

Trip scrubbed at his face with the heels of his hands.

"Okay, that sounds good. Do you know what time the buzzer goes off?"

Bailey gave him another confused look. Duh! She probably couldn't tell time yet. Trip snuck a glance at his watch. Five-forty-three. Cool, he'd gotten almost four hours of sleep. Ah, well, wouldn't be the first time.

"So what do you want to do until your mom wakes up?"

She sucked her lower lip between her teeth, again, just like her mother, and Trip felt another tendril of emotion wrap around his heart. "Do you read stories?"

He nodded thoughtfully. "I can do that. What would you like me to read?"

She hopped off the couch and dashed over to a plastic shelving unit beside the table. The bottom shelf was stuffed full of children's books. He took the moment to look around the room, something he hadn't really done in the tension of the night before. It was a little shabby, but scrupulously tidy and clean. Colorful throw pillows had been stitched together out of patches and lots of plants in vivid plastic pots brightened the small space. A hand painted wooden toy box sat invitingly in one corner next to a child-sized rocking chair. Framed photos of Bailey, and of Bailey and Beth together sat atop the small television and finger-paintings were taped to the front of the fridge. Overall, the effect was cozy and cheerful.

Bailey scampered back to the sofa with a dog-eared paperback in her hand and clambered up beside Trip. "This one, please."

"Looks good to me. Monsters are my favorites." His nephew Bobby was particularly fond of this story, so he knew it well. Even Trevor was already grinning when Trip read it to him. He stretched his bum leg out onto a footstool he'd pulled up and settled back into the sofa. He motioned Bailey up next to him so she could see the pictures while he read. After the first page of *Where the Wild Things Are,* he saw her mouthing the words along with him. She'd either memorized it, or was already on her way to being a reader herself. Why did that make him feel just a tiny stab of pride? He'd had nothing to do with it.

He did his best to entertain without making too much

noise. Beth needed all the sleep she could get, after such a rough night. So he snarled softly when the wild things roared their terrible roars and made a production of gnashing his teeth and showing his claws. Bailey's brilliant smile and suppressed giggles let him know he was on the right track.

Somewhere along the way his arm had gone around her tiny shoulders and she'd leaned into him, just like one of his nieces or nephews. They were having such a good time, he was actually sorry when the story ended.

When he closed the book, Bailey was beaming up at him. And then he heard the sound of applause. He looked up and saw Beth, once again bundled in the bathrobe from Hell, leaning against her bedroom door, a bemused smile on her face. He felt his own skin flush red.

****

Beth woke to the alarm even groggier than usual. She smacked it off and lay back on the pillow, forcing her eyes open. As her brain cleared, she remembered the events of the night before. The phone call, calling Trip, Fitz and Ree coming over, and the fact that there was a six-foot cowboy sleeping on her five-foot couch.

Oh, crap! Bailey didn't know he was there. Beth sat up and looked over at the other twin bed. Empty. Oh well, hopefully she hadn't woken him. Good thing Trip slept like a rock. But Beth wasn't looking forward to explaining this to her daughter.

She stood and pulled on her terry cloth robe, hoping to get some coffee started and a visit to the bathroom in before the explanations began. She stepped into the short hallway quietly, then stopped dead at the sight that met her eyes. Trip and Bailey were snuggled happily on the couch while Trip read Bailey her favorite story. And he was good at it too, the rat. She'd never gotten the monster's voices half so well. Bailey was grinning ear to ear and clapping her hand over her mouth to suppress her giggles, while Trip made faces and hand gestures to emphasize the story. Beth had to blink back tears at the picture they made. This was the kind of moment she remembered having with her father. The kind a little girl was supposed to have with her dad.

She knew she should just duck into the bathroom

and leave them to it. But she stood, rooted to the spot until they were done. Then she found herself clapping her hands, too choked up to speak.

Trip's eyes flew upward, he obviously hadn't even noticed she was there. His skin reddened, too, as if he were just a bit embarrassed to be caught having fun with a three-year-old. Then his expression softened to concern.

"Sorry if we woke you."

"You didn't. Didn't you hear the alarm go off?" She kept it set so loud you could practically hear it in the street. When they both shook their heads, she realized they'd been just that engrossed in the story, and she grinned.

"Goof balls." She turned toward the bathroom, calling over her shoulder. "Just for that, you can start the coffee."

Of course, she realized a few minutes later as she emerged, showered and slightly more focused, she hadn't bothered to tell him where anything was. She dressed swiftly and resigned herself to a glass of juice while she got the coffee ready.

When she turned the corner her jaw dropped. Bailey was seated at the table eating a bowl of cereal and sipping a glass of juice. Trip stood at the counter spreading butter on a slice of toast.

"Like that?" He showed it to Bailey, who nodded her approval. Then he cut it into quarters and handed it over on a folded paper napkin.

"Thank you."

Beth smiled at her daughter's precise politeness. While she liked to think it was her doing, in reality it was just Bailey's nature. In many ways she was three going on thirty.

"Hey there." Trip held out a steaming mug. "You look like you could use this."

He'd made the coffee. She could almost kiss him for that. Then she remembered the kisses from the night before and felt her face heat. She tipped her head down and inhaled the rich aroma of the coffee. He'd even added creamer, bless him. How did he remember this stuff?

"Sit." He pointed to a place set with a cereal bowl and a glass of juice. "Bailey says you like the wheat squares." He passed her the box of whole wheat cereal from the counter. "Toast?"

"Uh—sure." She took the cereal and poured a bowl full, too stunned by the service to do anything else. She honestly couldn't remember the last time she'd been able to just sit and eat breakfast without having to at least get up and get the dishes out of the cupboard. "How did you find everything?"

He grinned and hooked his thumb at Bailey as he removed another slice of toast from the toaster and buttered it. "My fabulous assistant over there. She really knows where everything is, even if she can't reach it yet."

Once the plate full of toast was ready, he set it on the center of the table and sat down next to Bailey, across from Beth and helped himself to the box of cereal. "As soon as we're done here, I'm going to duck over and take a shower at Fitz's place. I can steal a clean shirt from him while I'm at it, and pick up Trev. Then I'll be at the bookstore until Ree makes it in."

Not sure why he was telling her this, Beth kept eating, tipping her head to the side in silent query.

"Then, after I'm done at the shop, I'm going to pick up some heavy duty locks at the hardware store. Those things you've got on your door wouldn't keep out a determined flea."

"But my landlord—"

"Can cope. We'll express-mail him a set of keys, but there's no way you're spending another night here without new locks."

"I can't—"

"Not an option, Beth." His voice was soft, but rock-hard with determination. "My back and leg won't survive another night on that sofa. Either I change the locks, or I'm taking the pair of you back to my house until Fitz figures out what's going on. If you have a problem with the cost, you can take it off my next bill for the website."

What could she say to that? She would sleep better knowing the locks had been purchased sometime this century. She nodded and went back to her cereal.

Trip Hall was something else. He even did the dishes while she got Bailey washed and dressed. By hand, no less, since the apartment didn't boast a dishwasher. All in all, she was five minutes ahead of her usual time when she strapped Bailey into her car seat for the trip to the sitter's.

Trip leaned against the driver's door, blocking her way in. He held out his hand. "Keys."

She gave him a glare, but obediently pulled her house keys off her key ring and handed them over.

"Thank you." He shoved the keys in the front pocket of his jeans and stepped aside. Before she could get into her car, though, he leaned close and caught her shoulder with his hand. "One more thing."

"What?" She looked up at him, her hand still clutching the open car door.

"This." And once again he leaned down and captured her mouth in a kiss.

They were outside. On a public street. With Bailey in the back seat of the car. So this kiss was much more restrained than the ones from the night before. It was over in the space of three or four heartbeats. Beth still felt it all the way to her toes.

Trip's own breathing was a little shaky when he straightened and stepped away, she noticed with some degree of satisfaction. Whatever the hell was going on between the two of them, at least he was feeling it too.

"Drive safely," he murmured. He held the door open and handed her into the car. "I'll drop the new keys off at your office when I'm done."

"No!" She may have been a little more emphatic than she'd intended. Trip's left eyebrow flew upward. "Mitchell has a fit if we have any visitors at the office. Leave them with Ree or Shayna, and I'll stop by there on my way home."

Fitz leaned against the fender, his arms crossed over his chest and his body blocking her from closing the car door. She could see him ponder something for a moment, then he nodded. "I'll wait at the bookstore. See you at five."

Before she could answer, he stepped back and carefully closed the car door. She could almost swear he was whistling as he walked the few feet to his own vehicle.

****

"So, have an interesting night?"

Trip resisted the urge to slug his older brother. Instead he just glared at Fitz across his kitchen table and grunted. Ree and Trevor were still asleep, so the two brothers had a rare chance to confer alone.

"I assume if anything else had happened, you'd have given me a call."

"Yeah." He sipped at the coffee Fitz had offered. The rich Brazilian roast Fitz favored was a far cry from the pre-ground grocery store beans at Beth's place.

"I'm going to put new deadbolts on her door, and on the outside one today. If her landlord pitches a fit, I'm going to tell him you ordered it." Having the law on his side was an advantage he didn't often exploit, but he would if it came down to Beth's safety.

"Fair enough." Fitz raised an eyebrow. "Didn't know you two were so close."

"Don't." Trip glared over his coffee mug. "Just don't."

Fitz's smirk was downright smug, an expression only a brother could get away with. "Though I can't figure out what she'd see in the likes of you."

"Yeah, me either." Trip yawned, rubbed his eyes with a fist. "Not sure she does, to tell you the truth. Sounds like she had a pretty bad run the first time around. She's awfully gun shy."

Fitz nodded. "I'll find out more about that when she gets me that list. Some men should just be horsewhipped. But threatening phone calls—that doesn't sound like a three-year-old gambling debt to me."

"Me either. But she's convinced that's the only possibility."

"At least she says so. Frankly it sounds more like your garden-variety stalker. Which is something I really didn't want to deal with in Shirley. If somebody's gone off the deep end, there's no good way for that to end. And in a town this size, everybody is somebody's son, brother, or cousin."

"Yeah. And as long as that somebody sticks to the occasional phone call, I'd be fine with that. But this crap tends to escalate. I saw it happen in L.A. An actress I knew was damn near killed by her ex-husband."

Fitz nodded. "We'll keep an eye on things. I'll make sure my deputies cruise by her house more often. She going to get the phone line changed today?"

"She said she was. She's scared, bro. She'd have never let me stay if she wasn't." And didn't that just rankle like hell? He hated feeling like he'd taken advantage of her fear to further his own cause. Staying with her had been about concern. Kissing her had been about something else entirely.

"I'll see what I can find out," Fitz promised. "Meanwhile, go get in the shower if you're going to open the store. And thanks for that. Ree's feeling okay, but she's pretty wiped out by the end of the day. Sleeping in for a change will do her a world of good."

Trip nodded and stood. Fitz had already brought down a change of clothes so he headed off to the downstairs bathroom. While he cleaned up, Fitz brought down Trevor, and between them they got him fed and dressed. Thanks to the lessons he'd learned from his sisters, he always kept spare outfits in the diaper bag. Being a single parent was rewarding, but even with his big helpful family, it wasn't always easy. How much harder had it been for Beth? He couldn't begin to imagine.

****

At three minutes to five, Beth shut down her computer. Finally she could quit pretending that she was getting any work done. On her lunch hour she'd dug out her old records to make up the list of Daniel's creditors for the sheriff then emailed it over. Hopefully he could find a link there. She really didn't want to think it could be anything truly directed at her.

She packed up slowly and methodically, dragging out the moment she'd have to face Trip. Why was he insisting on getting so personally involved in this? Well, she guessed he'd sort of answered that question last night when he'd kissed her, but it still didn't make any sense.

She was still reeling from those kisses. The first one, full of fear and passion had scorched her to her toes. But today at the car—that one had been so tender and sweet it had melted her heart. One by one he was demolishing the defenses she'd worked so long and hard to build. The biggest blow had been watching him with Bailey this morning. Beth really didn't know how much more of this she could stand. What she'd felt in high school had been a crush, and it had still hurt when he'd overlooked her. How much worse would it be if she was foolish enough to actually fall in love with him?

"Leaving so early?" Donna, Mitchell's secretary sniped as she walked through the lobby. Beth was too caught up in other worries to even respond. It was after five. Donna was just being nasty. The older woman hated the fact that Beth was a fully qualified CPA, and not just another bookkeeper. In her mind, women were still supposed to be subservient background players, and a female accountant was an abomination against the natural order of things. Most days Donna drove Beth nuts. Today she was barely a blip on the radar screen.

Out the door and down the block. She paused at the hardware store to nod and smile at Mr. Eliot. No sign of Len today.

"Afternoon, Lizzie."

She didn't bother to correct the older man about her name. In a town like this, there would always be some people who held onto the past. She wondered if Trip had told him why he was buying locks. She felt her face flush as she hurried by. She didn't even duck into the salon to say hello to Shayna.

So when she walked into the bookstore and found Ree apparently alone, she was taken aback. Ree looked up from her computer screen and grinned.

"Have a seat. He'll be back in a minute."

"Oh?" She tried for nonchalance. "I couldn't just be in here for a book?"

Ree's laugh was warm and infectious. "Pull the other leg. Trust me on this. When one of the Hall brothers gets a bug up his butt, there's no shifting it. Trip's holding your new keys hostage. You might as well sit. He just ran home for more diapers and baby food."

Beth helped herself to a cookie and a cup of herbal tea that Ree always kept for customers then sat down in one of the leather sofas in the center of the store. Ree hopped down off her stool and joined her, her own mug of tea in her hand.

"So, you still enjoying married life?" Had she ever looked as starry-eyed and happy as Rhiannon did with Fitz? Or Allison with CJ, for that matter? Even Harper and her husband Jim, who'd been married for something like fifteen years. What was it about those Halls, anyway?

"Oh yeah." Ree's grin was ear to ear. "I never thought I would, you know. Never intended to take the plunge. But with Fitz—I just couldn't say no. And now?" She laid her hand across her tummy in a gesture recognizable to every woman on the planet. "Now I have everything I've ever wanted."

"Congratulations!" Both tea mugs had been set down on the table, so Beth leaned across to hug the other woman. They both blinked back tears when they pulled apart.

The two women chattered for a couple more minutes before a loud wail pierced the air from the open door in the rear of the shop.

Ree grinned and moved to stand. "Another country heard from."

"Is that Trevor?" He was the only infant Beth could think of who'd be napping at the shop.

Ree nodded as Beth followed her back to what she'd assumed was a storeroom. "I set the old storage area up as a break room-slash-nursery, for when Trip was working here during my honeymoon." She rolled her eyes. "And for later."

The freshly painted space contained two easy chairs, a playpen and changing table and a small television. "Very nice."

Trevor had pulled himself up to a standing position in the playpen. When Ree started to pick him up, Beth held out her hand. "Let me. I kind of miss the baby stuff now that Bailey's a little older."

Ree straightened and shrugged. "Go for it." She moved over to a half-sized refrigerator and took out a bottle of apple juice and a sippy cup, while Beth lifted the chubby body into her arms—and immediately wrinkled her nose.

"Somebody needs changing, huh?" There was a box of wipes and a stack of disposable diapers on the changing table, so she strapped the wriggling little boy to the padded surface and unsnapped his jeans.

"You ever think about having another one?" Ree asked.She leaned against the door jamb, probably watching out into the shop in case a customer came in.

Beth shrugged as she got to work changing the dirty diaper. “I'd have loved to have one or two more,” she admitted. “But Bailey was just two months old when I was widowed, so there wasn't time.” Not that she and Daniel had been sleeping together by then, anyway. “Besides, there were some complications with her birth. Scarring. The doctor said it's highly unlikely I'd ever be able to conceive again.”

“I'm so sorry, Beth.”

Beth didn't need to turn to know that Rhiannon's expression was warmly empathetic. Ree was just that kind of person. She was touched, all the same. “It could have been a lot worse. I have a healthy, happy daughter. That's more than many people can say. No reason to get greedy, I guess.”

She wrapped the dirty diaper and disposed of it, then snapped Trevor's tiny blue jeans back together. Without a thought, she hefted the now squirming bundle back to her shoulder and took the juice from Ree's outstretched hand. A smile lit Trevor's tiny face as he grabbed at the familiar cup, and drank thirstily. Beth's hands steadying the cup that he couldn't quite manage on his own yet.

“Why don't you two come on out here and keep me company?” Ree moved from the doorway back into the main area of the book store. She scooped up a small blanket and a set of stacking toys as she went. “Trip really should be back any minute.”

“I need to go pick up Bailey from the sitter,” Beth demurred. While it was nice of Trip to fix the locks for her, it was kind of annoying to have to sit here and wait. Why hadn't he just left the keys here? But he hadn't, so Beth followed Ree, then sat down on the sofa with Trevor in her lap. Ree set the blanket and toys on the rug in front of Beth's feet, then moved back to the register.

When Trevor finished his juice, Beth wiped his face carefully with a paper napkin. Before she finished, Trip strode in the door, a smile quirking the corners of his mouth and making his dimple flash. “Look who's here.”

“Like I had a choice?”

He stepped over to the sofa and immediately scooped Trevor up into his arms for a snuggle. Then without missing a beat, he leaned over and dropped a kiss on the top of Beth's head. "Ready?"

"Ready for what?" Beth heard the snottiness in her own voice as she stood and brushed the wrinkles from her boring gray suit. "Can I have my keys, please?"

"I need to show you how everything works." He bounded across the room to give his sister-in-law a hug. "Thanks for keeping an eye on Trev. See you Sunday at the ranch."

"No problem." Ree made a shooing motion with her hand, but her green eyes twinkled. "See you later, Beth. Have fun tomorrow at the carnival."

Beth was too bemused to resist when Trip nudged her toward the door with his shoulder.

"How about barbecued ribs for dinner?" Trip seemed to take spending another evening together for granted. But tonight was Friday. Girls' night. Before he got her out the door she had a brainstorm.

"Not tonight. Hey, Ree, want to join Bailey and me for our girls' night tonight? Girly movies, popcorn, and a big bottle of pink toenail polish? I was just going to pop next door and invite Shayna and her daughter to join us." It wasn't much of a lie. She had thought of it, just not until a second ago. But now she wondered why she'd never thought of asking her friend before.

Ree tipped her head to the side and considered for a moment. "I'd love it. Can I invite Allie to come too? That way these lugs..." She jerked a thumb at Trip. "Can get together for the poker game they've all been whining about. They can play at our house while we're at yours." She grinned at Trip's dumbfounded expression and winked conspiratorially at Beth.

Okay, her attempt to get some distance from Trip was taking on a life of its own, but it really did sound like fun. "Sure, the more the merrier, I guess."

"Great." Ree beamed. "I'll bring the chocolate ice cream. What time?"

"Seven thirty? Right after dinner? Bailey can't make it much past nine." She'd have suggested earlier, but Ree would want to have a little time with Fitz after the store closed.

Ree grinned. "Sounds perfect. You run next door and

ask Shayna while I call Allie."

****

Trip stared after Beth as she darted out the door. Then he turned to Ree who was already dialing the phone. "What just happened?" He was still recovering from the emotional punch of walking in to find Beth cuddling Trevor. The two had looked so perfect together, something deep in Trip's chest had clenched.

Ree paused her fingers and held the receiver loosely in her hand. "I think you just witnessed the start of a new family tradition. One that has your *friend* there right smack in the middle of it."

"Yeah." He shook his head again. "That's good, isn't it?"

Ree's chuckle was warm and friendly. "Got me. No real experience with functional family dynamics, remember?"

"Oh. Right." Ree had fit into his family so easily, and she radiated such contentment, it was easy to forget her own early life had been less than ideal.

"But," she went on. "I'd say she needs a little space tonight. So let her have it. She'll be fine with a whole roomful of women, including the sheriff's wife. I doubt any prank caller or petty voyeur is willing to take on your brother by hassling me."

"Not if he has half a brain, that's for sure."

Ree resumed dialing, and held up a finger to silence him while she conferred with Allison. She smiled widely as she hung up the phone. "Allie thinks it's a great idea. She and CJ are going to head into town shortly."

"And Shayna will be there with Molly." Beth breezed back into the shop, setting the silver chimes above the door tinkling. "She's sending Rick and Kenny over to your house, if that's okay with Fitz."

"Fitz won't care." Ree and Trip both spoke at once.

"And if I have company coming over, I really need to get home and straighten up." A slightly panicked look crossed Beth's face.

"Your apartment is fine," Trip assured her. He took her elbow with the hand that wasn't holding Trevor and pushed her gently toward the exit. "I promise, I cleaned up after myself when I installed the locks and motion-detector lights."

"Motion detectors?" She stopped cold and whirled on him. "Lights?"

Trip opened the door and nudged her out, smiling his goodbyes to Ree. "Nothing major. Let's go and I'll show you."

She sputtered, but she went. The chimes played softly as the door swung shut behind them.

"You want the tour first, or should we go pick up Bailey?"

She put both hands on her hips. "How about you just give me my keys and let me go get my daughter?"

"Nice try. Not going to happen, though. But if I tick you off a little more, you might actually get steam to come out your ears like in the cartoons." He wasn't even sure why he felt the need to provoke her, excerpt that her aggravation was better than the icy indifferent façade she kept trying to maintain.

She spoke through clenched teeth. "I think you're about to find out."

He shrugged. "Humor me. We'll go get Bailey, stop and get some take-out ribs for dinner at the Roadhouse, and when we get back to your place, I'll show you how the new locks work and help you clean up if you still feel the need. Then when the ladies start arriving, Trev and I will disappear. No sweat."

She shook her head. "It is so obvious that you're a youngest child. You clearly never learned the meaning of the word 'no,' did you?"

"Not true." They stood toe to toe on the corner next to the city parking lot, in full view of any downtown shoppers, but he couldn't care less who saw them or heard them. This was too important.

"About anything that isn't a safety issue, all you ever have to do is look me in the eye, say the word 'no.' That's it. If you really want me to go away, to stay out of your life, all you have to do is say so. And mean it. But I'm not going to give in about the locks or the lights. Even if there weren't a whole bunch of new feelings between us—feelings I'm pretty sure neither of us really has a handle on yet—I wouldn't budge about those. As a responsible friend and neighbor, I couldn't look myself in the mirror if

I hadn't done everything I can reasonably do to keep you and Bailey safe."

He paused, swallowed hard, and shook his head. "Today I happened to have the time and money to take care of those things. I hope they help you sleep a little easier tonight. I know I will. If you really want to pay me back, make me a pan of those lemon squares you used to make in high school. I haven't had those in years. We'll call it even."

She stared him down for a minute, then sighed and let her shoulders droop. She looked so young, so tired, he just wanted to gather her into his arms and hold her tight, but he knew she'd never let him. Not yet, at any rate.

"How the hell am I supposed to argue with that? Fine. I'll make up the lemon bars this weekend." Her expression softened and she reached out a finger and touched his cheek. "And thank you. I will sleep a lot easier tonight." Then she did the last thing he'd expected. She went up on her tiptoes and brushed a kiss against his jaw.

He resisted the urge to take her in his arms again. Baby steps, he told himself. That was the way he needed to proceed. Slow and steady.

So he gave her a wink and a grin instead. "Good. Glad that's settled. Now can we go pick up Bailey and dinner? I'm starving here."

Chapter Six

Beth was still shaking her head late the next morning as she tied the laces on Bailey's tennis shoes. Last night had been blissfully free of crank calls, and she had to admit that knowing motion-activated flood lights covered both entrances to the building had been a great comfort.

Trip had waited until Allie and Ree arrived, then taken Trevor over to his brother's house. He hadn't come back afterward, and Beth wished she wasn't so conflicted about that. Somehow she expected him to. He hadn't kissed her once before he left, and she wasn't sure how she felt about that, either. Was he just trying to keep her confused?

"Sit still for just another second, sweetie."

Bailey was fairly bouncing with excitement about the carnival. She'd never been to one before, didn't really know what one was, but she was thrilled all the same. Beth worried that what Bailey was really excited about was an entire day spent with Trip. She hadn't stopped talking about him all morning. This was exactly what Beth had feared, why she'd avoided dating. It wouldn't be fair to let Bailey to get attached to a father figure who wouldn't always be there.

"Is Trevor going too?" Bailey asked for the third time. She seemed almost as happy about that as about the carnival. Beth supposed that playing with Trevor was like having one of her dolls come to life.

"Yes, sweetie. Trevor is going with us, but he'll probably be in his stroller. He's too little to ride the rides."

"Can I push the stroller?"

"We'll see."

Beth checked her watch again. Ten minutes to twelve. Five minutes after the last time she'd looked. Jeez, she was just as bad as Bailey.

Which didn't stop her heart from speeding up when she heard the heavy, uneven tread on the stairs. She licked her lips and straightened the already neat pink bow on one of Bailey's ponytails.

"Mommy, open the door." Bailey was moving before the first knock sounded. Beth forced herself to take a deep breath and count to ten before she followed.

"Hi." Trip's warm greeting and wide smile made her stomach wobble. He was dressed for the warm, almost-summer weather in worn jeans and a rodeo t-shirt. A straw cowboy hat perched on top of his head. He held Trevor in one arm and reached down with the other to give Bailey's shoulder a squeeze. "Hey, short stuff."

"You look like you never left Shirley," Beth said with a laugh. "Total cowboy. Except for the tennis shoes. No cowboy boots today?" She picked up her oversized denim purse and slung it over her shoulder. Bailey didn't need a diaper bag anymore, but going out with a three-year-old still required a certain amount of supplies.

Trip's grin quirked sideways into a grimace. "There are orthotic inserts in the sneakers that I'm supposed to wear if I'm on my feet for too long. They don't fit in my boots. And these have more cushioning, or so the physical therapist keeps telling me. Some days I feel like an eighty-year-old man, but at least I'm on my feet, so I guess I shouldn't complain too much."

"Are you sure you're up for this?" The butterflies in her stomach disappeared in the wake of concern. The last thing she wanted to see was Trip hurting himself to show her a good time. It had been less than a month, after all, since she'd walked in and found him almost unable to move from his chair.

"I'll be fine. It's only a small local carnival. We'll hold off on Disneyland for a while, but I think I can manage anything Shirley has to offer."

Was that a slam? He looked so cheerful, she didn't think so.

He tipped his head toward the door. "Anything else we need? Or are we all ready to go?"

"We'll need Bailey's car seat." Beth picked up a zippered sweatshirt for Bailey and a light sweater for herself in case it cooled off later, then herded Bailey out the door Trip was holding open.

Once they were all strapped in, Trip drove the big vehicle out of town toward the county fairgrounds.

"Did you ladies have a good time last night?"

"We did." She'd had a blast last night, somewhat to her own surprise. How long had it been since she'd hung out with anyone other than Shayna? But last night she'd felt right at home. Shayna's daughter Molly had happily kept Bailey entertained, so the girl talk had been mostly of the adult variety.

The only thing that made her feel out of place with these women at all was the fact that she was the only one not married. But with both Ree and Allison expecting, the talk had soon turned to pregnancies and babies, and she had no problem fitting in with that conversation. She had only met Allison Hall in passing before, but the perky little math teacher had turned out to be a lot of fun. She was five months pregnant and just starting to really show. By the end of the night, enormous amounts of popcorn and chocolate ice cream had been consumed, and each of them sported a brand-new pedicure.

"How about you? Have fun at your poker game?" She wished she could keep the note of disapproval out of her voice, but after Daniel, gambling of any kind was a bit of a sore spot.

"Yep." He chuckled. "I was even the big winner."

"That's nice."

"So I'm sitting pretty today. Won a full ten bucks worth of quarters off of each of my worthless brothers and Rick Anderson."

Beth felt her own lips begin to twitch. "Ten whole bucks each, huh? High stakes game."

"Uh-huh. Family tradition. One roll of quarters is the buy-in. We each staked Kenny a buck so he could play a few hands, but then he got bored and decided to watch cartoons. Trevor, on the other hand, barely made it to the opening round before he conked out for the night. Besides, he was trying to chew on the cards."

"So are you buying us dinner with your massive winnings?" She should have known better than to worry. The Halls and Rick Anderson were all too smart to take their poker game seriously. And letting nine-year-old

Kenny play with the men for even a little while had been kind.

"Kind of hard to tote around that much silver," he admitted with a laugh. "So I traded it in on the folding variety. I'll roll them back up and we can use them again for the next game."

They sat in silence for a minute or two until Trevor started making noises in the back seat. Trip turned on the CD player, casting an apologetic look at Beth as the strains of a children's song came over the speakers. "Hope you don't mind. He seems to have a real thing for music."

"Fine with us. Bailey likes this group too." By the time they reached the fairgrounds, they were all singing along, though in deference to their ears, she was sure, Trip was singing too softly to be heard as more than a murmur.

****

When they reached the fairgrounds, Trip left Beth to extricate the kids while he opened up the tailgate and unloaded the stroller. It had a basket below the seat for the diaper bag and other essentials, so he wouldn't have to carry anything. His folding cane went into the basket, too, just in case. He wasn't using it so much for everyday errands anymore, but he wasn't sure about an all day walkabout.

"Okay, Trevor, here you go." Beth plopped Trevor into his seat and did up the seat belt. Trip added Beth and Bailey's jackets to the pile.

"Can I push the stroller?"

Trip looked down at Bailey, pondering the question. He hated to tell her no, but he was pretty sure the stroller with Trevor inside weighed just as much as Bailey did.

Beth sent him an apologetic look. "Sorry. She's been asking about that all morning."

"We'll figure something out," Trip promised. "But not until we get inside the carnival, okay? It's too bumpy out here in the parking lot."

Bailey nodded, and Beth bent down to straighten one of her ribbons. They made quite a picture together, those two blonde heads so much alike. They were both wearing jeans and t-shirts. Bailey's was pink with little ruffles around the edge, while Beth's was a simple scoop neck in bright purple. Beth had worn little or no makeup, and tiny silver stars dangled from her earlobes. She looked almost as young and fresh as her daughter.

They made their way through the parking lot and waited a few minutes in the admissions line, where they were given wristbands for the rides.

"How come Trevor doesn't have one?" Bailey's face scrunched up in outrage at the perceived unfairness.

"Because he's too little for the rides, short stuff." Trip chucked the little girl on the chin. "Those are for big kids like you. Trev has to wait a couple of years."

Serious brown eyes were still narrowed as if she was considering the explanation, then she smiled and nodded. "'Kay."

They started off with one of the kiddy rides, waiting in line with Bailey until it was her turn. When the operator tried to get her into the miniature car by herself, though, Bailey's courage deserted her.

"Mommy? Can't you come too?"

"Not on this one, baby. It's too small for me."

Bailey refused to go on alone, and they eventually gave up, pulling back from the line. Trip could see Beth's attempt at a pep talk was going nowhere, so he decided it was time to intervene. "How about the Merry-Go-Round?" he suggested. "We can all go on that one together."

Bailey cast him a doubtful look. "Trevor's too little."

"Nope. That's the one ride in the park Trevor can go on." The antique-style carousel had benches as well as horses. Trip could safely sit with Trevor in his lap.

"Okay."

The wait was short, and soon the four of them were boarding the carousel. Bailey picked out a white horse with two pink saddles. Beth lifted her daughter up, then climbed on behind her, while Trip watched from one of the ornately decorated benches with Trevor held securely in his arms.

Bailey was laughing by the time the music stopped. As soon as they exited the merry-go-round, she started pulling Beth toward the next ride. This time Trip and Trevor waited on the sidelines until the teacups had finished spinning, then they all moved on to the next ride.

"Oh! Not that one, Bailey. Mommy really doesn't like

heights."

Bailey gazed longingly at the Ferris wheel, then looked up at her mother with big sad eyes. "Please."

It was a small Ferris wheel designed for families, but Beth had gone sheet white. How had he forgotten Beth's fear of heights? She'd absolutely freaked when they'd tried to make her go off the high dive in high school swimming class. Trip remembered standing at the bottom of the ladder talking her down when the coach had finally relented and let her climb back down instead of jumping. He nodded toward the stroller. "Why don't you sit this one out, Mom? Bailey can ride with me. This is one of my favorites."

Beth's eyes widened then fluttered shut as she sighed with relief. "Would you? Thanks."

"No sweat." He crouched down and laid his hand on Bailey's shoulder. "How about it, short stuff? Can I go with you while your mom watches Trevor?"

Bailey's thoughtful expression was unbelievably adorable. It was all he could do not to kiss that wrinkled little brow. Then she smoothed it out and smiled at him. "Okay."

He straightened and took her hand to get in line. When they strapped the seat belt over their laps, she crushed herself close against his thigh, and Trip wrapped one arm around her, holding her tightly, even as the metal restraining bar locked into place.

"You ready?"

"Uh-huh." Her tiny fingers were white on the bar as the car started to rise.

"Look, there's your mom and Trevor." With his free hand he pointed over her shoulder to where Beth was waving at them, then he waved back. Distracted from her fear, Bailey lifted one hand and waved too. Then she spotted the carousel and pointed that out, and from then on the ride was one of excitement and discovery. She was still chattering when they rejoined Beth and Trevor on the ground.

"Hey, Uncle Trip!"

He'd just reached to take a squirming Trevor from Beth's arms when he heard his niece, Jessica, call him. He turned around to find Harper and Jim standing there with all four of their kids.

"Hey guys." He shook hands with his brother-in-law and gave his sister a hug. "You both know Beth Corcoran, right?" Five years older than Trip, Harper wouldn't have known Beth very well when they were younger.

"Only vaguely," Beth demurred. "I haven't been much of a social butterfly since I moved back to Shirley."

"Well, I imagine this one keeps you busy." Harper beamed at Bailey and tapped her youngest daughter, a grinning redhead who had just turned three. "This is Lucy. Maybe we can get these two together to play some time."

"We were just about to go get some lunch," Trip interjected. "Want to join us?"

The two oldest were more interested in the rides, but Harper and Jim were more than ready for a break. While Jessica and Rainey took off on their own, the others moved over to the concessions area and snagged a big table. After getting everybody's preferences, Trip and Jim went to stand in line, leaving Beth and Harper with all four kids. Trip hid a grin as they went. Beth clearly felt odd being seen on a date, but Trip knew Harper wouldn't let her withdraw back into her shell.

"You know you're in for the inquisition tomorrow." Jim's grin was wide on his friendly, freckled face. "Your sister's never gonna let this one go."

Trip nodded. "Ree and Allie already have their noses in it. Harp would have been all over me after ten minutes with them anyway." As the eldest of the girls in the family, Harper kept a very maternal eye on Trip.

"You're the only one left for her to match-make with," Jim added. "Figure your bachelor days are numbered whether you like it or not."

"We'll see." A month ago, that thought would have terrified him. Now it didn't sound bad at all. "Seems like the lady has some say in the matter."

****

By the end of the day they were all exhausted. The bright sunshine had warmed the fairgrounds, so everyone was sweaty and dusty after a long day of lines and rides and games. Even Bailey was cranky.

Beth's exhaustion was emotional as well as physical.

It seemed like every time they'd turned around, there was someone clapping Trip on the shoulder and shooting speculative glances at the two of them—no, *four* of them—together. Beth wanted to scream, or at least paint a big sign on her forehead that said, "No I am not Trip's new girlfriend." They were just friends, damn it. So why had the entire freaking town been grinning behind their hands all day? Even Trip's family—besides Harper and Jim, they'd run into CJ and Allie later—had acted like Beth was an acknowledged part of the landscape.

"Don't wanna go!"

"Bailey, I said it's time to leave."

"One more ride." This time she looked up at Trip. The little manipulator knew she already had the big man wrapped around her finger. Trip was such a soft touch. Beth had seen it earlier when he'd spent half an hour throwing softballs to win giant teddy bears for both Bailey and his little niece, and a stuffed dog for Trevor. Bailey's pink bear and the blue hound dog now rode piggy back on Trevor's stroller. *He'll give in*, Beth predicted. *And he's already limping*. He needed to go home and put his leg up far more than Bailey needed another trip on the carousel.

"Nope, short stuff. Mommy said it's time to go, and what Mommy says goes."

Beth stopped in her tracks and stared. He'd said no. Amazing. She watched, saying nothing as Bailey's lip trembled. Here came the tears. He'd never be able to resist those. She resigned herself to one more ride.

Trip squatted down and wiped away a tear. "Aww, don't cry, darlin'. There's lots more fun things to do another day. Next weekend I'm opening up the swimming pond. How about you and your momma come out to my house next Saturday and help me try it out?"

"But I want to go on the merry-go-round."

"Sorry. No can do. Time for this old cowboy to get home to bed. In fact, I'm almost too tired to push the stroller the rest of the way to the truck. Think maybe you could help me out with that?"

Ooh, he's good. That was the one prize Bailey had wanted all day, but had forgotten about in the excitement of the carnival.

Bailey scrunched up her face and nodded. "Your leg

hurts, doesn't it?"

"It does," Trip admitted. "I could sure use your help."

"Okay." She wiped away her tears and turned around to grip the handle of the stroller, which was on a level with her chin. Trip stood behind her and put his hands on either side of hers.

"Together, right?"

"Yep," Bailey agreed.

Trip counted to three and then they pushed the stroller carefully toward the exit. Beth followed along, blinking back tears of her own.

"So how about it, Mom? Barbecue and pond party at my place next Saturday?"

The rat! There was no way she could turn him down in Bailey's hearing. She rolled her eyes and nodded. They made it to the car and got the kids into their seats without further discussion. Five minutes into the drive home, she turned around to realize both children were sound asleep.

"I guess we really wore them out."

Trip laughed. "I guess so. But I think everyone had fun. I know I sure did."

Beth's heart jumped into her throat. But she couldn't lie to him. "Me too. Thanks for taking us."

"Thanks for going. It wouldn't have been any fun with just me and Trev. I wouldn't have gotten to ride the Ferris wheel."

He pulled the SUV into her driveway and killed the engine. Neither child stirred. "I'll carry Bailey upstairs for you," he offered.

"No. I can tell your leg has had enough. We'll manage."

"Beth—" He caught her shoulder when she moved to exit the truck. Then his hand moved up to her cheek and turned her to face him. He kept his voice low, so they wouldn't disturb the kids. "I had a great time today. With Bailey. But also with you. I'm giving you fair warning that I'd like to see you again."

She tried to laugh it off. "It's a small town. We see each other all the time."

"That's not what I meant and you know it."

She did, but she wasn't sure she could acknowledge it

with words. Not yet. Part of her was still sure that as soon as he was fully recovered, mentally and physically from his accident, Trip would be off to bigger places and flashier women than Shirley, Wyoming and Beth Corcoran.

He leaned in gently and placed a tender kiss on her lips. When she made an involuntary sound he pulled her face closer, deepening the kiss, and sliding his tongue inside.

Whatever she'd been about to say, whatever she'd been thinking, it all disappeared the minute Trip's mouth touched hers. Beth's body went limp, except for her hands, which wrapped around his shoulders and neck, holding him in place while she kissed him back for all she was worth.

Trip groaned out loud when he finally pulled his face away from hers. "One of these days we're going to have to find a way to do that without the kids around."

Beth nodded, even though she knew that would be a very bad idea. Too bad her body didn't agree.

He opened his door and got out of the truck, coming around to her side before she'd even gotten herself together enough to move. He stood beside her opened door and held out her hand. "Keys."

She tilted her head and looked up at him.

"It's going to take two trips at least, with Señor Bear over there. And I want to make sure the new locks are working properly. I'll take up the stuff, then you can take Bailey up when I get back."

Beth started to argue, then shrugged. At least this way he wouldn't hurt himself carrying Bailey up the stairs. She handed him her keys and climbed out behind him as he moved to get the bear and their jackets from the back end. When he stepped into the house, she woke Bailey and gently maneuvered her out of her car seat and onto the porch.

"Okay, everything looks good. You two have a good night." Trip limped down the stairs and back to the porch. He leaned down and hugged Bailey, then straightened and pulled Beth into his arms. "I'll call you tomorrow, darlin'."

Feeling Bailey's interested gaze, Beth didn't argue.

Trip's kiss this time was soft and brief, no longer than the one he'd dropped on Bailey's ponytail, but somehow sizzling all the same. Then before she could do more than whisper, "Goodnight," he was gone, down the steps and back in his truck.

The two of them stood there and watched the SUV move down the tree-lined street.

"Mommy?"

"What, sweetie?"

"I like Mr. Hall. And Trevor."

"So do I, Bailey. So do I."

"Can we keep them? Please?"

Chapter Seven

Trip stood by the corral fence outside CJ's barn the next day, waiting for the interrogation to begin. Fitz and Ree were waiting until everyone arrived to make their big announcement. Even though it wasn't much of a secret anymore, Trip figured the excitement over the new baby would take the heat off of his relationship with Beth. Fortunately, CJ was the most diplomatic of the bunch, and he was the one Trip was currently standing next to, talking horses.

"Yeah, I'll bring over Patton and Mack tomorrow in the trailer, no problem," CJ said. He crossed his arms over his chest, leaned back against the fence rail and ran an assessing eye over Trip's leg. "You sure you're up to taking care of them?"

Trip nodded. "Got the okay from both the physical therapist and the doc, as long as I don't overdo it." He'd spent a good portion of last week making sure the long-disused stable at his cabin was operational. Now he was looking forward to being able to ride on a regular basis. Not only would the exercise be good for his body, he didn't know of anything better for clearing the mind.

Then another idea popped into his head. "Don't suppose you know anyone with a pony for sale?"

"Trev's a little young for that yet, isn't he?" The corner of CJ's mouth quirked up into a grin.

Trip shrugged. He wasn't thinking about Trevor yet, and CJ knew it.

CJ nodded, not bothering to repress his big-brother-knows-all smirk. "Take Frodo. He's just eating his head off here. We won't need him for a couple years yet. Harp and Willa's kids have ponies at home. No real need to keep one here just for visits."

The long-haired Shetland pony would be perfect for Bailey, even if he really did resemble the hobbit that

Rainey had named him for. "Fine. I'll keep him at my place until I find one for sale."

The crunch of tires on gravel interrupted the conversation and they both turned to see Willa and her husband Al pulling up to the house in their big SUV. When the vehicle stopped, the two adults climbed out, followed by their pair of year-old black Labradors, who frolicked around the driveway wagging their tails while Willa and her husband each opened a back door to unstrap an equally excited child from a baby restraint or booster seat.

Trip and CJ moved to greet the new arrivals, swapping hugs with Willa and toddler Becky, ruffling five year old Bobby's hair and scratching furry black ears. The door on the farmhouse opened and more children began to spill out to see their cousins, followed by Allie and Harper.

"Hey, who's this?" Trip turned at CJ's query, to see Willa helping another large dog down out of the truck. It was golden brown with a black nose and ears and a white tip on its tail. It looked like maybe a shepherd mix, but the most notable feature was the missing front leg. Once on the ground, it moved easily enough, hobbling around to sniff the driveway, and wagging its tail at all the people.

Willa sighed, and scratched the dog's ear when he came over to lean against her leg. "This is Gonzo, Al's latest adoptee. He was in a car accident with his owner, who didn't survive. None of the man's family would take him, so he's with us until we can find him a permanent home." Willa and Al were both veterinarians and had taken over Al's father's practice a couple hours away.

Trip held out a hand toward the black-tipped muzzle. Gonzo rewarded him with a friendly lick, and Trip patted the dog's big head. "How old is he?"

"About two," Willa replied. "He's been great, but three beasts this size is more than I want to deal with every day along with the two kids."

"I'll take him." The words were out of his mouth before he even knew he was going to say them. "As long as you think he'll be safe with Trevor."

"Becky adores him, and he's been incredibly gentle with her." Willa grinned and tipped her head toward the labs who were wrestling with Mike and Bobby in the dusty gravel driveway. "More so than those two goofballs."

"Great." Trip knelt and looked the dog in the eyes. "Well, Gonzo, you want to come home with me?"

Gonzo slurped his huge tongue across Trip's face.

The humans all laughed. "I think you can take that as a yes." CJ noted. "Two horses, a pony, and a dog, all in one day. Sounds like you're finally settling in."

"Hey, they've always been my horses." He'd bought the pair of Appaloosa geldings several years ago, making a deal with CJ for their care. The ranch hands had free use of them for work, and Trip had his own mounts to ride when he'd visited home.

"I know, and the pony is only a loaner." CJ chuckled and moved toward the house. "Still, I'm just saying it's nice to see you finally settling down."

"Settling down?" Willa's sharp dark eyes turned on Trip as they both walked up the steps to the porch. Living farther away, she was a little less in the loop than her siblings, though Trip knew she wouldn't let that stop her from grilling him before the day was over. She was the second youngest, so Trip had been the only one she could safely rag on growing up. Unfortunately, she'd never quite broken the habit.

She was also the only one who had really known Beth in school. As soon as Harper had informed her about Trip's "date" for the carnival, over dinner, she turned a speculative gaze on Trip and pursed her lips. Then of course, the whole story of Beth's threatening phone calls had come up.

"So you're sure she's really a widow? Usually the first place you look for a stalker is the ex-husband." CJ toyed with his water glass as he spoke, black eyebrows knit together over his dark brown eyes. Harper was the only other sibling to share Trip's blue eyes.

"Last time I checked, I was still the cop in the family." Fitz threw a wadded up paper napkin at CJ. "And yeah, I checked. She's definitely a widow. Daniel Corcoran was a pathetic excuse for a husband—"

"Pathetic excuse for a *man*," Trip interjected.

Fitz nodded. "That too, by all accounts. But he is a dead one. And I checked into his gambling debts. There were too many to count, but they were all local and all small-time. None of them would come after the widow three years later, in another state."

"Damn it." That meant it was personal, and Trip felt the chill all the way to his bones. "You have anything else to go on?"

Fitz shook his head. "Nope. Not one thing to prove it was anything more than a crank call. Has she gotten her number changed yet?"

"Monday morning, according to the phone company."

"I'll make sure that whoever's on patrol keeps an eye on her place. Don't suppose you can convince her to stay with a friend for a while?"

"Nope. Or with me." Trip sipped his coffee and grimaced despite the rich taste. "Not that I really thought *that* would be happening any time soon."

"Just a side note here bro, but isn't she, like, the first woman you've dated in the last year?" That was CJ, the former lawyer, frowning at him.

Trip shrugged. "More or less." This was where he got warned to take it slow. *Yeah, like I have a choice about that one.*

"That doesn't mean it's a rebound relationship," Willa argued, surprising Trip with her support. "They were friends from first grade all the way through high school. Always figured there'd be something going on there one of these days. At least until they both left town."

"You're kidding?" Trip stared across the table at his sister.

Willa shrugged. "Seriously. There was always this weirdly close vibe between the two of you. I was surprised you never dated in high school. Instead you were always playing around with bimbos like Pam Davenport and DeeDee Robinson."

Exactly. Because with the bimbos there had been no chance of anything getting serious and making him want to stay in Shirley. But he wasn't going to say that to his siblings. They didn't need any more ammunition.

It was kind-hearted Ree who came to his rescue. "Maybe it just wasn't the right time," she suggested softly. "Maybe they both needed to go out in the world for a while, become the adults they were meant to be. I like

Beth. She's smart and kind and she works really hard to provide a good life for her daughter."

No one could refute that, and no one was going to argue with Ree today anyway. With her fair skin glowing and her red curls shining around her, she looked like a Botticelli angel. The whole family was thrilled at the thought of having yet another niece or nephew to spoil. Not to mention that Fitz would take anyone apart who even looked at her crosswise. The middle Hall brother had spent most of the day with a goofy grin on his face. Just like the one on CJ's. Once again, Trip couldn't help but wish his own life had turned out more like theirs.

****

Later that night, Trip sat in his living room watching baseball, while Trevor cruised around the room, pulling himself up on the furniture. He'd be walking soon, Trip realized, with a little jolt of panic. His son was growing up at a rate Trip could only pray to keep up with.

It was late, Trevor should be asleep, but he'd had an extra long nap, then slept in the car on the way back from the ranch. Trip was too tense to sleep. The big mutt, Gonzo, seemed happy with his new surroundings. He'd thoroughly explored the house earlier, and now lay curled up at Trip's feet, thumping his tail happily whenever Trip reached down to scratch his ear. He and Trevor hit it off right away, so it looked like Trip had officially become a dog owner. He was adding roots, he noted, making this house he and Trevor lived in into more of a home, and it felt good. Even if it was only ever the two of them, they were still a family, and this was still a home. Tomorrow CJ would come with the horses, adding yet another sturdy root to this small but sufficient family tree.

He was pondering that happy thought when the phone rang, startling Trevor, who plopped down hard on his bottom and began to wail. Trip started to go to his son, ignoring the phone, but Gonzo got there first, limping across the room at what looked like light speed. He plopped down on his haunches and bathed the little boy's face with his drooly, oversized tongue. Trevor's wails quickly morphed into giggles.

Chuckling himself, Trip reached the phone seconds before it switched over to voice mail. "Hello?"

"Trip?" The voice was Beth's and she sounded scared. Trip's entire brain and body immediately went on alert.

"What's wrong?"

"He called again."

Trip swore viciously, hoping Trevor didn't hear over his own squeals of delight as he played with the dog. "What did he say?"

"Not much. Just a lot of heavy breathing. But then..."

She broke off and he could hear the tears in her voice. Immediately he tucked the phone under his shoulder and started reaching for his tennis shoes.

"Then what, sweetheart?" He tied his shoes then stood to go get Trevor. Looked like they were going for another drive tonight.

He heard her inhale deeply then exhale in a long slow sigh. "No-nothing. He just...called me a name, that's all."

"Have you called my brother?"

"Yes."

"That's good." Trip sighed, then leaned down to pick up Trevor. "I'm on my way. I'll be there in fifteen."

"No." There was no waver or hesitation in her voice this time. "Your brother is sending over a deputy, who is supposed to make sure everything is secure. There's no point in dragging you and Trevor all the way into town. It's not like there's anything you can do, anyway."

No, nothing except see for himself that she was all right, and keep watch to be sure she stayed that way.

"I mean it. Tomorrow's a work day, for me anyway, and if you come over, it will be hours before I get to sleep."

And if he didn't, he'd be awake all night worrying and wouldn't get to sleep at all. "So why did you call?"

She sighed deeply. "I guess I just wanted to hear your voice. I wanted to talk to someone who..."

"Who what?" He coaxed with his voice, wanting like crazy to be able to take her in his arms. Then he carried the phone back to his recliner and forced himself to sit back down. If she didn't want him to come to her, he wouldn't, even if it killed him.

"Someone who doesn't think of me like *he* does."

"Well, whatever he said couldn't have been good, so I'd say it's a sure bet that I think of you differently. Don't let him get to you, Beth. There isn't a damn thing wrong with you. Whatever this guy's problem is, it's his, not yours."

Her chuckle was rusty, but he had to give her points for trying. "See, that's what I meant. You always know what to say to make me feel better. It's that Hollywood charm of yours."

"Beth, whatever I tell you has nothing to do with charm, Hollywood or otherwise. It's the simple truth. I knew it in school, and I know it now. You're one of the best people I've ever met. Smart, strong, gorgeous… Whatever this asshole told you, he was wrong."

"Yeah, if I'm so gorgeous, then explain why I caught you kissing Pam Davenport at the prom. When you were my date."

Huh? Trip bobbled the phone. Where the hell had that come from? Had he? He searched through the memories. Oh, hell, he had. He pressed the heel of one hand to his forehead, wishing they didn't have to talk about this on the phone. He groveled much better in person.

"That's what I thought." She seemed to take his stunned silence as an admission that he'd been lying about her appeal. Then her voice softened. "It's okay, Trip. I know I'm just an ordinary kind of girl. I certainly wasn't interesting in high school. There's no need to pile on the baloney."

"Christ!" Trevor looked up at Trip's expletive, and Trip forced himself to calm down. "What happened prom night had nothing to do with you being uninteresting, and everything to do with me being a horny teenage idiot." Uninteresting, hell! Just the memory of her in that strapless dress had his jeans getting tight.

And that had been the problem at the time. He'd been eighteen and so turned on by his date he could barely stand up straight. He'd known better than to try to put the moves on Beth, so he'd snuck off into the corner to try and talk Pam, whose date was a mindless jock, into helping him relieve the tension. Not one of his more noble moments. It hadn't worked. Even though he felt like he was turning blue, his rebellious body hadn't been interested in Pam, and she'd left him, moments after the kiss Beth must have seen, her mocking laughter ringing in his ears.

"It never occurred to me in a million years that you'd have seen that, Beth. I'm profoundly sorry. It was a crass and stupid thing to do."

"Well, you'd only taken me as a pity date anyway, so it's not like I had any claim on your attention."

"Pity date?" Where had she gotten that idea? Sure, he'd just asked her as a friend. He'd done that mainly out of self-protection. Most of the girls in this town considered prom night sacrosanct. If he'd asked any of them, he'd have wound up in Shirley with a ring on his finger by the next fall.

"Oh come on, you know that's what it was. Sort of a thank you for helping you with trigonometry."

Trip shook his head, even though he knew she couldn't see it. "Boy do you have that wrong. I was an idiot back then, but not that big of one. I took you because you were my friend, and I wanted to be with you. And because, truth to tell, I couldn't stand the idea of some other guy putting his hands on you."

She snorted. "Which explains the kissing another girl part. It's okay Trip. We *were* friends. It just—hurt a little at the time, that's all. No one had ever kissed me like you were kissing her, and I was a little jealous."

"Sweetheart, if I'd thought, even for a minute, that you'd have let me kiss you instead, things would have ended a whole lot differently." Hell, their whole *lives* might have ended up differently. But then there would have been no Trevor, and no Bailey. Maybe, just maybe, things did happen for a reason, like Ree had said.

"Aww, there you go again, saying just the right thing to make me smile. Thanks Trip. For being my friend then, and now."

He had a lot of ideas about ways to make her smile, and most of them required skin-on-skin contact. "You're sure I can't come over there?"

"I'm sure." A lot of the strain had gone from her voice, so he supposed he'd managed to do something to help. "Now I hear the deputy ringing my doorbell, so I'm going to hang up. Have a good night, Trip."

"You too sweetheart. And if anything else happens,

you call me, okay. No matter what time of the night."

"I will. Scout's honor."

Trip laughed. "That's right, you were a Girl Scout, weren't you? Great. Now I get to go to sleep fantasizing about you in a little green uniform."

Her giggle warmed his heart. "Goodnight you big goof." He could almost see her roll her eyes. Yeah, too bad he hadn't been kidding.

****

She couldn't believe Trip had actually managed to make her laugh. Just talking to him for a few minutes had given her the fortitude to talk to the deputy, a fresh-faced young man by the name of Tim Turner. He checked out the house and the yard, tested her motion-activated lights, and suggested she get a dog. When he was done, she dutifully double-checked the locks behind him and made her way back up to her apartment, then double checked the locks on the inner door as well.

She was too wired to sleep and didn't want to wake Bailey by tossing and turning in the bedroom, so she turned off all but one dim lamp and curled up on the sofa, an old afghan over her feet.

How had life gotten so complicated so quickly? One day she was just a working mom with too much to do and no money to do it, and then suddenly she was going to carnivals and being kissed and being targeted by some sort of weird stalker. She knew it all had to do with Trip, but she couldn't figure out why, still couldn't make the connection.

She should tell him to back off, that he didn't have a place in her life. Bailey was already growing attached to him, and Beth knew it was only going to get worse. Just like she was getting all too fond of Trevor, as well as his irascible father. It felt so good to hold a baby again. Walking through the carnival, it had been so easy to pretend they were just another family—mommy, daddy, and two beautiful children. Beth had needed to remind herself continuously that it wasn't real. Even sitting there, having lunch with his family had seemed so natural, so normal. It would be far too easy to let herself believe in the fantasy.

But she just couldn't bring herself to brush him off.

Not when every so often she saw that vulnerable glint in those sky-blue eyes. She knew first-hand that being a single parent wasn't easy, and she knew that for Trip, learning to live life at less than full throttle had to be a major adjustment as well. Besides, every time she tried to push him away, he always managed to say exactly the right thing to change her mind. She knew it was crazy to let him hang around, but she just didn't have it in her to tell him no.

So where did that leave her? And what did Trip have to do with the lunatic who'd called her a whore over the phone tonight. Ha! If the bastard only knew. She hadn't had sex since Daniel died—since well before, if the truth be known. Four years and counting. And in all that time, no one had made her want to until Trip. Now every night she went to bed restless and achy, longing for the kind of fulfillment she had good reason to believe didn't really exist. Sex with Daniel had been pleasant, even fun, but never the Earth-shaking experience she'd read about in the romance novels she borrowed from Shayna. So why did her traitorous body keep wanting to find out how it would be with Trip?

****

She was tired and cranky the next day. She'd fallen asleep on the couch, earning herself a stiff neck and sore lower back. Then when she'd finally gone to bed, sleep had eluded her, and she'd ended up tossing and turning all night, trying like crazy not to disturb Bailey. One day soon, she vowed, she was going to have to find a two-bedroom apartment.

She squinted at her computer, rubbing her tired eyes. The motion caused one of her contact lenses to pop out, and she scrabbled around on her knees, searching for it on the floor.

"Looking for something?" The snide voice belonged to Donna, the office manager from Hell. The puritanical old coot always seemed to be looking for ways to get Beth in trouble.

Beth grimaced, glad her face was turned toward the floor. "Contact lens."

Donna's only response was a long-suffering sigh. "Whenever you're finished..." She let her voice trail off on the implication that Beth was deliberately wasting precious office time.

Beth found the errant lens and picked it up. She'd have to clean it before she could put it back in, which would require a trip to the restroom. She stood, picking up her purse from under her desk in her empty hand.

"Was there something you needed, Donna?" She finally looked up at the older woman and was surprised to find her holding a small package wrapped in green florist's paper.

"This arrived a few minutes ago." Donna gave a disapproving sniff. "I should remind you that this is a place of business, and personal deliveries are *not* expected during office hours." She plopped the package down on Beth's desk so hard Beth winced, afraid whatever was inside would be smashed. Then Donna stormed off, back to her cave—er—office.

Beth wavered for just a second then decided she'd better be able to see when she opened the package. She dashed off to the restroom. After five minutes of struggling, she gave up on the contacts, and put them in their case, and rammed her plastic framed glasses on over her now-bloodshot eyes. Then she hurried back to her cubicle.

The sweet scent of roses wafted up from the paper-wrapped bundle. Beth's stomach did a flip. There were only two people who might have sent her flowers. Either they were from Trip, or they were from her stalker. Either choice was scary in its own way.

Just in case they were from the stalker and needed to be used later as evidence, she used her scissors to carefully cut away the staples holding the paper closed at the top. Bright yellows and greens showed in the opening, so at least the flowers were fresh, not beheaded or dried out. That boded well, didn't it? The she used a binder clip as forceps to pull the card from its little plastic prongs.

"Have a great day. Trip and Trevor."

She wasn't sure how much of her sigh was relief and how much was exasperation. But there was a little thrill under her skin as she sat down and carefully peeled back the dark green tissue. No one had ever sent her flowers at work before. In fact the only flowers she'd ever gotten had been from Shayna. Once when Bailey was born and again for Daniel's funeral.

She should be annoyed at Trip for getting her in trouble with Donna, and she'd have to remember to tell him not to do it again, but…

Oh! The green glass vase held a small but lovely arrangement of yellow roses interspersed with cheerful daisies. Did he know daisies were her favorites? She leaned down and inhaled the heady aroma. *Gorgeous!* Beth set the arrangement carefully on a corner of her desk where she'd see it every time she looked up from her work. To heck with telling him not to do it again. Some things were worth getting chewed out by Donna.

She wasn't the least bit surprised to find Trip waiting for her outside the office at five-fifteen. She was surprised to see him standing there alone.

"Where's Trevor?"

"Back at the house. My nieces are watching him. Well, to be honest, Rainey is probably reading or outside somewhere. Jessica's a great babysitter, though."

"With three younger siblings and all those cousins, I'm not surprised." She remembered the girls from the carnival, and could understand Trip trusting them. Jessica was fifteen or sixteen, right? Old enough to babysit for a few hours. She hadn't known Trip had horses, but she ignored that remark for the moment. "So what brings you to town on your own?"

He shot her a wicked grin. "Well, it's all part of my evil plan. I was hoping we could pick up Bailey and drop her off at my house with the girls. Then maybe we could go have dinner somewhere. Just the two of us."

It sounded wonderful! It also sounded dangerous. Beth hesitated.

"Come on," he wheedled. "It's just dinner. I promise to have you and Bailey home no later than nine o'clock." His voice turned serious as he took her hand between his. Beth tried to ignore the looks they were getting from other pedestrians on the sidewalk. "How long has it been since you had a night out?"

The night she'd had dinner with Shayna, then gone to Trip's house to apologize. A month? In all honesty, it seemed like just yesterday, yet in other ways it seemed like forever.

"I promised the girls pizza, if that's okay with Bailey."

Bailey loved pizza, and she didn't get it often. Beth wavered. Oh, heck, she hadn't even thanked him for the flowers yet. She nodded. "Fine. Let me go home and change, then we'll go get Bailey."

Trip fell into step beside her, his fingers lacing automatically through hers. He waved at Shayna through the window of the beauty salon, and Shayna just waved back, didn't even bat an eye, drat her. Ree did the same as they strolled past the book store. The only person they passed who didn't smile and wave was Len Eliot at the hardware store. He just grunted. Well, maybe now he'd get the message and quit asking her out. Len was a nice enough guy, she supposed, but he always smelled like he'd been drinking, and that was an instant turn-off.

Of course Trip followed her all the way upstairs.

"Did the phone company get your line changed?"

"Umm-hmm." She showed him the brand-new caller identification machine, and handed him an index card on which she'd written her new, unlisted phone number. "The only people who will have this are you, my boss, and Shayna."

"Good." He slipped the card into the back pocket of his jeans. "I still wish you'd consider staying with someone else until Fitz figures this out. Like maybe with me." His arm slid around her waist and she allowed herself to lean into his comforting warmth.

"Not gonna happen, Hall." She wished her voice carried a little more certainty, but it was hard to be determined when he was so close beside her and he smelled so good.

"If you say so."

His voice was soft and husky. The hand that wasn't on her waist reached around to land on her shoulder, gently turning her body toward his. The thought of resisting him didn't even cross Beth's mind. She laid both her hands against his thin western-cut shirt and looked up into his eyes, letting him see that she was waiting for his kiss.

Heat radiated through the fabric beneath her fingers,

and she felt the groan rumble through his chest as his lips lowered to hers.

"Beth."

Surely the little whimper she heard couldn't have come from her own lips. She rose up on her toes to meet him, hungry for a taste.

His big hands flattened against her back, holding her right up against him as his lips moved against hers. She could feel the impressive bulge in his jeans pressed up against her and her own body softened in response.

He tasted of coffee, of peppermint, and of something indefinably Trip. His tongue traced the inside of her mouth, exploring each ridge and crevice with a mixture of reverence and urgency than made her knees wobble. Beth's arms wound up and around his neck, both for support and to allow her to press her suddenly heavy breasts against his muscled chest.

"Beautiful."

Beth wanted to cry when he pulled his lips away from hers, but she'd barely had time to gasp for breath when she felt the gentle glide of his mouth slide along her cheek to her ear. Oh, lord! The way he made her feel as he nibbled on the lobe and stroked with his tongue was probably illegal in half a dozen states.

It was the first time they'd been alone, with no children. That thought hovered in the back of her mind even while she allowed him to slide her linen-blend blazer down off her shoulders. She didn't even notice it hit the floor, just gloried in the sensation of his big warm hands sliding down the bare skin of her arms. Her blouse had little cap sleeves that didn't impede him at all. Neither did the buttons, not for long. Then he slid the blouse off as well, and Beth went still.

Her body wasn't horrible, but it was far from perfect, as Daniel had reminded her on a regular basis. She never had time to work out, and there were stretch marks from her pregnancy.

"Beautiful," he murmured again. She started to contradict him, but then his fingers were running reverently above the plain cotton cups of her bra, and she forgot how to speak.

Somehow, he'd maneuvered them over next to the

sofa. He eased himself down on the cushion, still holding onto her, so she ended up standing in the vee of his thighs. She trembled while he kissed his way from her neck down to the swell of her breasts, his hands cupping her less-than-generous flesh. When he thumbed her nipples through the threadbare cotton, she couldn't suppress a moan.

"Have to taste you." His words were thick and raspy. He didn't wait for her to respond, just reached around to unsnap her bra then tugged it away and tossed it to the floor. Then he groaned. "God, Beth!"

Her knees bucked when he took her distended nipple into his mouth. Gentle hands at her waist held her steady and she leaned her own on his shoulders for support.

He nuzzled her softly then moved his lips to the other breast, treating it to the same thorough attention as the first. Somewhere in the back of her mind, warning bells were clanging, but she ignored them. This was Trip! After all these years of loving him from afar, she finally got to find out what if felt like to be the woman in his arms. She might berate herself later for giving in, but for right now, she was determined to enjoy every second, and make a memory that might have to last her a lifetime.

He slid his hands down over her backside and down her thighs, then up beneath her skirt. She cursed the pantyhose that kept his touch from her skin, didn't even think of protesting when he hooked his fingers in the waist band and drew the hose down past her knees. When they dropped to her ankles, she kicked them off along with her pumps. A flash of pink told her that her underwear had gone as well. Her skirt was ruched up around her waist—otherwise she was completely naked while Trip was still fully clothed. She should have been embarrassed, but all she could do was feel.

His hands slipped up along her inner thighs as gentle as a whisper. He continued the onslaught on her nipples, tonguing and suckling the sensitive flesh. When his fingers reached the curls between her legs, she cried out, and her knees gave way completely. He caught her as she collapsed, turning her to lie along the couch, while he sat between her knees.

"God, Beth!" Her name had never sounded better. He

leaned over her and covered her breasts with his hands while his lips kissed a blazing hot trail down her belly. She watched his dark head dip lower, but when he reached the apex of her thighs, her head fell back against the cushion and her eyes fluttered shut. She almost wept when his warm hands left her nipples, but then he used them to gently part her legs and lowered his head between them. Beth gripped the rough fabric of the ancient couch with her fingers, holding on for dear life as his tongue traced the seam of her cleft and dipped inside.

She felt her hips rise off the couch to meet his caress, knew her breathing had gone shallow and fractured. It had been so long since anything had felt this good. Maybe forever. Then he drew the beaded bundle of nerves between his lips and sucked, and Beth's world exploded.

"Trip!" She cried out his name as her body convulsed. He held her hips still, stroking her with his tongue until the pulsing faded into a soft warm glow. Then he moved away, though she didn't think he'd gone far. Through the haze of aftershocks, she heard the snaps on his shirt, the slide of his zipper. Then there was a tearing sound. She opened her eyes to see him rolling a condom onto his erection.

Her eyes went wide and she swallowed hard. He was big, a lot bigger than Daniel had been. But this was Trip, and after the gift he'd just given her, there was no way she was going to deny him. Instead, she opened her arms, offering herself wordlessly as he lowered himself between her splayed thighs.

"You sure?" His voice was little more than a ragged whisper.

Beth had to wet her lips and swallow before she could get the word out, but she was pretty sure her blinding smile was all the answer he needed. "I'm sure."

"Thank God," he murmured, then lowered himself over her to take her lips in a kiss that was hot, hard, and hungry. She dug her fingers into the warm solid muscles of his shoulders as she kissed him back. The taste of herself on his lips made her ache even more, and she shifted her hips restlessly against him, straining to get that hard length inside her—even if she wasn't totally sure it was going to fit.

He held his body over her with one hand while he used the other to position himself. She could hear the wet slapping as he ran his erection through her curls to moisten the tip before slipping just a tiny bit inside. He paused there at her entrance, and looked down at her face. She'd never seen those clear blue eyes blaze so intently before, and it thrilled her beyond belief that right now it was all for her.

He held her gaze as he pushed slowly inside. It felt so good, but at the same time, it hurt just a little. He must have seen that on her face, because he went slowly, pulling back then edging further forward just a little bit each time. Beth had never felt closer to another human being in her life. By the time he was fully imbedded inside her sheath, tears were leaking from the corners of her eyes, and they weren't from the stretching.

"You okay?" He held himself perfectly still, the tip of him nudging her more deeply than she'd ever been touched.

Beth just nodded and smiled. He still looked worried, so she made her lips and vocal cords form the only word she could think of. "Perfect."

Chapter Eight

Holding still was about the hardest thing Trip had ever done. Beth was so soft, so sweet, and so incredibly tight, it was all he could do not to go off like a rocket. He knew her too well to think she'd been with any other man since her husband's death, and he was so damned honored it almost made him want to cry. Watching her come apart in his arms, he'd nearly gone over the edge himself, coming in his jeans like an over eager teenager.

Finally Beth took pity on him and flexed her hips, letting him know it was all right to move. He tried to keep it slow and gentle, but it wasn't long before both of them were straining against one another in perfect rhythm. When Beth shattered around him, milking him with her tight inner muscles, Trip followed. Her name was on his lips as he came, a hoarse cry straight from his heart.

He held himself deep inside her until the spasms had passed for both of them, peppering her face with kisses while her fingers dug hard into his back.

He saw the moment reality intruded on sensation. Her eyes flew wide and her whole body stiffened beneath him.

"Bailey! What time is it?"

Trip checked his watch, which was the only thing he still had on. "Five thirty. Let's get cleaned up. We'll be in plenty of time to get her from the sitter's." Reluctantly, he eased his body up off of Beth and off the couch. His leg was sore, but the rest of him felt so damn good he didn't care. He reached out a hand to help Beth up off the couch, then stood aside while she darted into the bathroom.

He winced as she slammed the bathroom door in his face. That didn't bode well. He picked up his jeans and briefs, and waited. When Beth dashed from bathroom to bedroom, wrapped in a towel, he ducked into the bathroom himself to get rid of the condom and wash up.

His elation dried up like a mud puddle in the August sun. To him, what had just happened had been wonderful—an almost spiritual experience. Obviously not so to Beth. She'd thrown her defenses back up and reinforced them before Trip could even get his pants on.

He was back in the living room pulling on his boots when Beth emerged, dressed in a high-necked cotton blouse and a pair of baggy cargo Capri pants.

"Ummm—thanks." She picked up her clothes which he'd folded neatly and stacked on the table. "I—uh—think I'll have to pass on dinner, though. Too much work to do tonight."

Oh crap! She was going into full-blown denial, and Trip didn't have the faintest idea of what to do about it. He nodded slowly. "Okay. How about tomorrow?" He'd pay his nieces a salary to wait at his house every night to baby-sit, if that's what it took.

Her eyes were wide, panicked. "Ummm—probably not. I mean, I..."

He couldn't take it anymore. He crossed the room and put both hands on her shoulders. Her trembling touched something deep inside, made his throat swell. He leaned down and kissed her soundly on the lips.

"I'm not going to argue Beth. You want some space tonight, that's fine. You can have it. But I'm not going to let you blow me off. What just happened wasn't a fluke. It was special, important. We've got some serious talking to do, too. We took precautions just now, but I know first-hand that those can fail. Before I walk out that door, I need you to promise me that if anything happens, I'll be the first to know. I couldn't live with not knowing—not again."

"We're safe." Her gaze softened.

She was too empathic not to understand, too honorable not to agree.

"I'd never do that to you, Trip. That much I can honestly promise."

"Okay." He kissed her again, this time just a gentle brush of his lips against hers. "Then the rest can wait. I'll call you sometime tomorrow, all right?"

She nodded and went up on her toes to press a soft kiss on his cheek. "Thanks." Then she stepped back, pulling herself out of his arms. He felt the loss immediately, a pain almost on par with the one in his leg right after the accident.

****

The sense of loss and restlessness plagued Trip all night and the whole next day. Teresa was in the house keeping an eye on Trevor, so Trip spent most of the day out working in the stables to get them ready for the horses and pony. He smiled at the thought of putting Bailey up on Frodo's sturdy back. She'd had a five-minute pony ride in a circle at the carnival and had been thrilled. How much more excited would she be to learn to ride for real?

Gonzo limped gamely beside Trip as he moved about the tidy building. The stable had been empty since Trip's grandfather had passed, but thanks to Harper and Jim, it was still in good shape. All it needed was cleaning. Trip had a load of hay delivered that morning, and there were bags of feed in his truck. The physical labor felt good, but he couldn't get Beth off his mind.

Should he stop by tonight? Or just call? He knew she needed space, but he didn't want to give her enough to let her completely rebuild her defenses. He had no doubt she was terrified of the heat that flamed between them. Hell, he was kind of scared of it himself. But he was even more frightened of letting it slip away.

He decided he had to see her in person. It would be just too easy for her to say no over the phone. But he didn't want to scare her.

Unfortunately, by the time CJ and Allie arrived with the trailer holding two horses and a pony, it was almost five. It was well past dinner time when they got the animals settled, and Allie was starved. It would have been rude not to take the two of them out to dinner as a thank you. Then they all had to stop and visit with Fitz and Ree while they were in town. Before they were finished talking, Trevor had gotten cranky, and Trip knew there was nothing to do but take him home and put him to bed.

So after he got Trevor put to bed, he settled for a phone call. When he reached her answering machine, he spoke slowly, giving her time to get to the phone. No answer. *Damn it!*

Was she not home, or just avoiding him? He didn't much like either idea. Should he try her cell phone, or would that just look desperate? He ended his message with, "Please give me a call when you get in," and hoped she would.

****

Beth knew she was being a coward. She'd ignored Trip's messages for two days, even though it was kind of mean. Given the situation with her caller, he was justifiably worried. She just honestly couldn't think of a single thing to say to him.

So now she lay in bed, unable to sleep for the second night in a row.

Making love with Trip had been—incredible. What he'd made her feel was so far above anything she'd ever felt before, she had a hard time even reconciling the experience with reality. Surely it had all been a product of her overheated imagination. She'd dreamed of Trip since she was a teenager. Why couldn't he have been like everything else in her life and failed to live up to her dreams? Instead he'd exceeded them. And all with a ten-minute quickie on her miserable couch. What would it be like to have a nice soft bed and all the time in the world?

A suspicious tickle made her throat twitch, and her nose was getting stuffy. *Great!* Now on top of everything, she was fighting a cold. Didn't that just figure?

Grumbling to herself, she climbed out of bed and trudged to the bathroom. If she didn't take an antihistamine now, she'd never get to sleep, and she'd be utterly miserable tomorrow.

She took a cold tablet and drank a glass of water, then crawled back into bed to wait for them to work. When she finally did fall asleep, her dreams were full of Trip.

The heat he generated was amazing, her entire body felt like it was on fire. His hand landed on her shoulder. Instead of caressing, though, he began to shake her. And it couldn't be his voice shrieking, "Mommy! Wake up!"

Beth jerked awake to find Bailey looming above her bed.

"Mommy, wake up! Fire!"

"Fire?" Cold medicine or no, that word brought Beth into full consciousness. She could smell smoke and hear an ominous crackle. Oh, God! The heat she'd been feeling wasn't just part of her dream, or an incipient fever. Her home was actually on fire!

She jolted out of bed. There was an eerie yellow glow coming through the bedroom window. She pulled Bailey toward the front door. Not so much glow through the windows on the front. That was good, right? *Think, Elizabeth!* She laid her palms against the door to the stairs to see if it was hot.

Okay, no more so than the rest of the house.

"Bailey, stand back while Mommy opens this."

Obediently, Bailey ran back behind the table. Beth turned the knob gingerly, expelling the breath she'd been holding when she saw that there were no flames or smoke in the stairway.

"Come on, baby, let's go!" She scooped Bailey up in her arms, then, automatically grabbed Bailey's sweater and her own purse off the hook by the door. When they got out, she could use her cell phone to call the fire department.

They dashed down the stairs and out to the lawn. Beth lifted Bailey into her arms for a hug. "You okay, sweetie?"

Bailey nodded. "Is it going to burn down, Mommy? I want my bear back."

"I don't know, sweetheart." Beth finally looked at the house. There were flames and smoke, but not as much as she'd expected. The fire seemed to be confined to the back porch area—right under the upstairs bedroom!

She handed Bailey her sweater. "Put this on, then we're going to go across the street and sit on Mrs. Milliken's porch, sweetie." As soon as they were across the empty street, Beth shooed Bailey up to the neighbor's porch and dug her cell phone out of her purse.

****

Once again, Trip was having a sleepless night. Why was Beth determined to ignore him? Even worse, what could he do about it?

He was in the sun room lifting weights when the phone rang? Beth? It was nearly midnight, so odds were it wasn't good news. He hoped she hadn't gotten another phone call.

He wiped his sweaty hands on the hem of his t-shirt and picked up the cordless phone. "Hello?"

"Trip, it's me." Fitz's voice came over the line. His tone was serious, his professional cop voice, and Trip began to panic in earnest. "Jim and Harper will be at your house in a couple of minutes. You're going to want to be dressed and ready to roll. Harper will stay with Trevor."

His panic level rose. Something was very definitely wrong. "What the hell?"

"Before you freak out, let me say that everybody's fine. But Beth Corcoran's apartment is on fire."

"What?" He heard his voice rise to a shriek, but he started moving on autopilot, heading up the stairs for clothes, shoes, and his wallet.

"Jim's a volunteer fireman, so he's on his way in. Since your place is on the way, he'll pick you up."

"I'll be ready to go. You're sure she's okay? Bailey?"

"I'm sure. They're sitting in my truck down the street."

"Thanks. See you in a few."

Fear burned in his gut. How had this happened? Were they really okay? He waited at the front door for Jim, barely nodding to Harper as she moved past him inside, squeezing his shoulder as she passed.

"We'll be fine here," she assured him. "Jim's mom is with our kids. Give me a call when you know what's up." Jim's mother had an apartment off the back of their ranch house, so Harper always had a built-in babysitter.

Neither Trip nor Jim spoke a word on the way into town, but Trip spent the whole ride praying to anyone he thought might be listening.

****

It couldn't have been more than two minutes later that she heard the sirens. About that time, the neighborhood began to rouse to the commotion. Soon, the fire trucks showed up, along with Fitz Hall, out of uniform, who swiftly extricated Beth from her well-meaning neighbors and installed her in his king-cab pickup truck, parked well down the street. Shayna's husband Rick, a volunteer fireman, stopped by to invite her and Bailey to spend the night with them, but she just smiled and didn't respond. She sipped the cup of tea from Mrs. Milliken with one shaky hand while she stroked Bailey's flaxen hair with the other.

What if Bailey hadn't woken?

She shuddered at the thought.

More volunteer firemen arrived, and the blaze seemed to be mostly under control, but Beth couldn't really tell in all the commotion. Fitz had taken her car keys and some helpful deputy had moved it out of her driveway, so she wouldn't lose her car, even if she lost everything else. Hopefully her fire-proof file cabinet would hold. It would be nice to have her insurance paperwork, their birth certificates, and a few of Bailey's baby pictures that she'd tucked in a box in the bottom drawer. And her computer back-up disks. Thank God she had renter's insurance.

A dark-colored pick-up with a red bubble light screeched to the curb in front of her, and Trip leaped out the passenger side before it even fully stopped. Seconds later he wrenched open the door of his brother's truck and scooped both Beth and Bailey into his arms.

She forgot all the reasons she was supposed to stay away from him. He was here when she needed him, and she allowed herself to grip his shoulders, holding him tight.

"Thank God you're both all right." His words were whispered into her hair. One of his hands gripped Beth's shoulder, and she could see the other one flattened on Bailey's back, as if he needed to touch both of them to reassure himself that they were unharmed.

"We're fine," she murmured into his chest. "Nobody got hurt. That's all that matters, right? The rest is just—stuff."

"Amen to that!" There was a quaver in his voice that matched the one in her own.

Beth scooted sideways on the seat to make room for Trip, pulling Bailey up onto her lap. Trip shifted more fully into the cab and sat, still not releasing his hold on Beth. The fingers of his other hand grazed Bailey's cheek in a gentle caress. "How you doing, short stuff?"

"I'm okay," Bailey said seriously. Her lower lip

trembled. "But Señor Bear is still inside. Is he going to be all right?"

"I hope so, sweetie," Beth told her daughter. The truth was she had no idea if anything would be left by the time this was over.

Trip looked out the windshield for a moment. "Actually, it looks like the fire is about done. You want me to go see what I can find out?"

No! She didn't want to let go of the comfort he brought just by sitting here next to her. But Beth nodded. She needed to know.

Trip dropped a kiss on the top of her head as he slid back out of the pickup. "Be right back." He strode off into the night. All he needed, Beth thought, almost hysterically, was a white horse and a matching white cowboy hat.

Her gaze followed him. The firemen did seem to be winding up their hoses and stripping out of their protective gear. She glanced fearfully over at the house. It was still standing. From this angle she couldn't see much else. She shivered, even though it was warm in the car. Then she looked down and realized she was wearing nothing but her pajamas—a cartoon t-shirt and a pair of stretchy cotton shorts. Fitz Hall had handed her a blanket when he'd put her in his vehicle, but it was only draped loosely over their legs.

She tried to convince herself it didn't matter. Trip had seen her in less, and Fitz wouldn't notice a woman other than Ree if she danced naked on his kitchen table. Besides, even in her pj's, Beth was probably wearing more than most people did at the beach.

Part of her brain recognized that she was obsessing over something trivial in order to avoid thinking about the fire, but that knowledge didn't stop the shaking. Beth bit her lower lip, trying to forestall the tears that were filling her eyes.

She managed, until Trip returned. When he sat back down in the truck, she flung herself against his chest and let herself cry. Bailey, squished between them, wriggled until she found breathing space. Wouldn't you know it? Her little arms were wrapped around Trip's waist too. He shifted Bailey onto his lap and held each of them with one strong arm. "It's going to be all right," he soothed. "Everything is going to be fine."

He wished he knew what to do, what to say to help them through this. He'd never been as terrified before as he'd been the whole way here, hoping they weren't hurt. Now he couldn't seem to stop touching both of them, just to convince himself they were both alive.

"The damage isn't too bad," he told Beth when her sobs had quieted. He lifted the fleece blanket Fitz kept for emergencies and wrapped it more securely around both of the females. "It looks like the fire started on the back covered porch, and you called it in early enough to keep it mostly contained. There'll be water and smoke damage, but most of your things should be salvageable." Except for books and photos, he thought. Two things he knew they cherished. "You won't be able to go inside for a while though. First the fire inspectors have to go through it, then the safety inspectors. It might be a week or two."

"Great. A week or two with no clothes, no food, nowhere to sleep." She sniffled and wiped her face with a corner of the blanket.

Trip brushed a damp strand of hair back off her face. "We'll take care of it. One day at a time. You can get through this, darlin'. I'll be right here beside you all the way."

That made her start sobbing again, and she buried her face back into his chest. Damn, what had he said wrong?

"Where's Trevor?" Bailey's tiny voice interrupted his thoughts and Trip squeezed her tiny shoulders.

"At home in his bed. His aunt—that's my big sister Harper, you met her at the carnival—is staying with him until I get home."

"Okay." She patted Beth's arm. "Don't be sad, Mommy."

"I-I'm not sad, baby." Beth made a visible effort to get herself together and smile at her daughter. "I'm just tired,"

Bailey screwed up her face in confusion, then she shrugged and looked back up at Trip. "Can we go back to bed soon? I'm awful tired."

"Soon, sweetheart. You're going to have a sleepover

at my house tonight, but we can't go just yet. If you want to, you can stretch out on the back seat and snooze there for a while."

Bailey looked up at her mother for approval. When Beth nodded, Bailey willingly climbed over the seat back and settled down on the rear seat using one of Fitz's spare jackets as a pillow. Still sniffling, but more composed, Beth leaned over and arranged the blanket around Bailey. As soon as she turned back to Trip, she pierced him with a glare he could see even in the dim light filtering in from the streetlamps.

"Your house?"

Trip crossed his arms over his chest. "Yeah. My house. You got a problem with that?"

"You don't have to do this. We do have other options, you know. Shayna has a guest room she invited us to use. Same with Mrs. Milliken across the street and the Gundersons next door. Even Len Eliot offered to let us use the empty apartment over the hardware store for as long as we need it."

He looked down his nose at her and shook his head. He wasn't giving her the option. Not this time. "My house."

Beth stared back for a moment, then she seemed to just deflate in front of his eyes. "Fine." She crossed her arms over her chest, too, and he saw her shiver.

"Christ, I'm an idiot." She was in shock, which meant her body temp would be down. He whipped off the hooded sweatshirt he'd tossed on and handed it to her. She gave him a wan smile and immediately pulled it on.

"Thanks."

Out of the corner of his eye, Trip saw Fitz approach.

"I'll be right back." He climbed out of the truck to talk to his brother, closing the door to keep out the evening breeze.

"Well?"

Fitz just shook his head. "It looks like arson—sloppy arson at that. Found a gas can and some bits of cloth on the back porch."

"Shit!" It was the prank caller. It had to be. Only now he'd been officially upgraded to stalker status.

"She have somewhere safe to sleep tonight? I can

assign a deputy to keep an eye on her for a day or two."

"She's going home with me."

Fitz didn't even blink. "Okay. She can come in and file a statement sometime tomorrow. But there are a couple of questions I need to ask her right now. Then you can take her car and head home."

"Fine." Trip opened the door and held out his hand. Beth took it and climbed out, nodding at Fitz.

"Did you see or hear anyone around the house before you noticed the fire?"

Beth shook her head. She didn't pull away from Trip, which he was glad about. She didn't protest when he laced his fingers loosely through hers either.

"I was asleep," she admitted. "I'd taken a cold tablet, so I was really out of it. Bailey woke me up and told me there was a fire."

"Do you mind if I ask her what she saw or heard?"

Beth bit her lip, but shook her head. "I trust you," she murmured to Fitz. "Go ahead."

"I'll get her." Trip let go of Beth's hand and moved around to the back door of his brother's truck. He lifted Bailey out of the back seat, still wrapped in the blanket. He shook her gently and called her name to wake her, then carried her to the front of the truck, under the streetlamp where Fitz and Beth still stood.

"Hi Bailey, remember me?" Fitz asked kindly.

Bailey yawned and nodded. "You're the sheriff."

"That's right. I'm also Trip's big brother. I wanted to tell you that you did a great job tonight. Waking up your mom and getting out of the house was a really brave thing to do."

Bailey just looked up at him soberly, her hand clenched in Trip's T-shirt.

"How did you know there was a fire, Bailey? Did you see something, or hear something?"

Bailey scrunched her little face up for a minute, then nodded. "The lady told me. She woked me up and told me to get my mommy 'cause the house was burning down."

"Lady?" Fitz asked. Trip and Beth shared a befuddled glance.

Bailey nodded again. "Lady with black pigtails and a white dress. Like my doll from Col'rado."

"Your Native American doll?" Beth gave Bailey a funny look. Trip and Fitz shared a gaze of wide-eyed astonishment. It couldn't be. Could it? Fitz shook his head a fraction of an inch while Trip shrugged.

"Yeah. My 'Merican doll. Only she sort of looked like you, too." Bailey pointed at Fitz. "She said I had to get up and wake up Mommy 'cause of the fire. Then she disappeared."

Bailey looked up at her mother. "Mommy, do you think she was my garden angel? Miss Lisa says we all have garden angels. Even if we don't have a garden."

"Garden—do you mean guardian angel, honey?"

"Yeah. Garden angel. You think that's who she was?"

Beth shook her head. "I don't know sweetheart, but I'd definitely say she was a miracle."

"Yeah." Trip agreed.

Fitz nodded. "Okay, folks, time to go get some sleep. I'll have my dispatcher call your office in the morning and let them know you won't be in tomorrow," he told Beth. "You need to get some rest."

"Okay." Beth looked dazed, but she nodded at Fitz. "Thanks."

"No problem." Fitz handed Beth's car keys to Trip. "Let him drive okay? You still look kind of shocky."

Beth just nodded one more time and led the procession over several houses to where her station wagon was parked. Trip tucked Bailey into her car seat, then let Beth fuss with arranging the blanket around her daughter, while Trip got into the driver's side and started the engine.

They didn't speak the whole way back to Trip's house. Bailey's story kept replaying over and over in his head. Had he ever told Beth about his family's ghost legend? Of his many-times-great-grandmother Singing Bird? Supposedly to this day she showed up now and again to help members of the family when there was danger. Both Allie and Harper claimed to have seen her, and since Ree's car accident last spring, Fitz got a funny look on his face whenever she was mentioned. Ree too, come to think of it.

If it had been Singing Bird, did that mean Bailey and Beth were supposed to become members of the family?

They would if Trip had anything to say about it. One thing tonight's scare had done is convinced him that he was absolutely and irrevocably in love with Beth. He was damned attached to her daughter as well. Yeah, if he had any say in the matter, they'd both be changing their names to Hall in the near future.

Chapter Nine

Harper was waiting for them when they reached Trip's house. She fussed over both Beth and Bailey for a few minutes, plying Beth with tea and Bailey with cocoa until her husband arrived a few minutes later to take her home.

Beth still wasn't sure she should be here, but she knew Trip wouldn't have taken "no" for an answer.

Once Harper and Jim were gone, Beth slumped in one of the big leather chairs with her tea, while Bailey slurped hot chocolate and scratched the three-legged mongrel who seemed to have joined the household since their last visit.

Trip smiled at the girl and the dog, then turned to Beth. "That's Gonzo. Willa and Al needed to find him a home after his owner died."

Ah. That made sense. "Well, at least your vet bills should be cheap."

Trip chuckled at her weak attempt at a joke. They both watched until Bailey set down her mug and yawned.

"Time for bed, I think," he said, picking up Bailey.

Beth glanced at the clock. Three a.m.! She was exhausted, but far too wired to go back to sleep. She stumbled along beside Trip like a zombie as he carried Bailey up the stairs, and into a pretty, feminine bedroom with white furniture and a full-sized bed covered with a pink patchwork quilt. A few stuffed animals sat on the built-in window seat. Beth moved to pull back the blankets, then Trip set Bailey gently down on the bed.

"Is this your room?" Bailey rubbed her eyes while Beth helped her off with her sweater. Then she lay back against the pillows, looking up at Trip.

He chuckled, bending down to kiss Bailey's forehead. "No, this was my mom's room when she was a little girl, then my sisters used to use it when they came to visit my grandparents."

He handed Bailey a well-worn Raggedy Ann doll off the window seat. "I'm sure she gets lonely over there by the window. Think you could help keep her company tonight?"

Beth blinked back tears when Bailey nodded and clutched the doll close. "Where's mommy going to sleep? There's only one bed."

Beth opened her mouth to speak, but he beat her to it. "I've got another room for your mommy to sleep in. Don't worry she'll be fine."

"'Kay." Bailey yawned and snuggled into the pillow, clearly ready to go back to sleep.

"Goodnight, short stuff." Trip leaned down and kissed Bailey's cheek. Then he brushed a hand across Beth's shoulder as he stepped away. "Meet you in the hall, he murmured, then ducked out the door, leaving Beth to say goodnight.

"You okay, baby?" She sat down on the edge of the bed. "If you need me, just yell. I'll leave my bedroom door open."

Bailey yawned again, and nodded. "'Kay."

A long hug and a couple of kisses later, Beth turned off the overhead light and stepped out into the hallway, leaving Bailey's door ajar just a few inches. Trip leaned in the doorway of another room off the hallway, waiting.

Beth's heart sped up, just looking at him there. So handsome, so concerned. So unbelievably sexy. She shook her head as he took a step toward her. "I could really use a shower."

"No problem."

"Actually a bubble bath would be even better, but I'd settle for a shower."

One eyebrow lifted and he smiled. "I've got a better idea."

"Oh?"

He started down the stairs. "Follow me."

Mystified, she followed. Gonzo looked at them, then turned and slipped back into the room where Bailey slept. "Will he be okay in there?"

Trip nodded. "He's been standing guard in Trevor's room at night. He's very protective of kids, apparently."

She followed him through the living room and out to what had been, in his grandparent's time, a screened-in porch. Now she saw it had been converted into a year-round room, with heavy timbers and thick, insulated glass. Work-out gear was clustered at one end of it, while a large spa filled the far corner. Beth's knees nearly went out from under her at the thought of soaking her aching body in all that bubbly hot water.

"This is new," she said. She walked over to the hot tub and dragged her hand through the water. "You keep it on all the time?"

"No." He came up behind her and began kneading her shoulders. "But I was working out when my brother called, and I'd fired it up for after I was done. I sort of forgot to turn it off when I high-tailed it out of here."

Oh lord, his hands felt like heaven on her shoulders. If he didn't stop she'd fall down soon. "I don't exactly have a swim suit."

"I've seen you naked," he reminded her. His breath caressed her ear as he whispered. "Or you can leave your clothes on if it makes you feel more comfortable. I've got sweats or a T-shirt you can wear later."

She knew she shouldn't give in to the seduction in his voice. But right now his touch felt like the only thing solid and safe in her world. She gripped the bottom of her t-shirt and pulled it off over her head, then shimmied out of her shorts. She heard his sucked in breath and felt him go still behind her. She turned, lifted a hand to him.

"Throw those away," she said. "I'll never be able to wear them again."

"Anything you say." He took her hand, raised it to his lips, then led her over to the steps and handed her into the spa. The hot water swirling around her legs was a shock, though a pleasant one, and she gasped, then sank down onto the bench.

"Can I join you in the tub?" Trip's jaw was taut. She could tell he was keeping his impulses under control by sheer strength of will.

Beth licked her lips and swallowed hard. "Please. I need you to hold me, Trip. I need to feel alive."

"God, yes!" He toed off his tennis shoes, then stripped off his T-shirt and jeans. She watched every movement, taking visual stock of his body in a way she hadn't taken time for when they'd made love on her couch.

The scars covered most of his thighs and crisscrossed his arms and chest. Some where white lines, others vivid red welts, puckered and angry. Her heart broke at the thought of the pain he'd endured, what he must have overcome to be walking again. Then her eyes landed on his erection and she gulped. No question in the world about what he had in mind. She forced herself to look up, into his gorgeous blue eyes.

His smile was blinding, even more so for the hint of vulnerability in it. Never in her wildest dreams would it have occurred to her that she would hold the power to hurt him in any way.

He stepped down into the hot tub and lowered himself to the bench beside her. She turned toward him, a tremulous smile on her face.

"Beth." Her name was a benediction. He leaned forward, cupped her face in both his hands and lowered his mouth to hers.

The kiss started out gentle, but soon moved to frantic. He pulled her onto his lap, his lips never leaving hers. His tongue alternately plundered and withdrew, enticing her to follow, exploring him the same way he explored her. His hands slipped down her body, one wrapping around her waist, while the other found her breast and rasped the nipple with one calloused thumb.

"Trip!" She arched her back, pushing further into his hand. He caught the pebbled bud between his forefinger and thumb and rubbed, while his mouth traced a line down the side of her throat. Without even thinking about it, she reached down between their bodies and caught his heavy shaft in her hand, stroking the smooth skin and the solid flesh.

Trip groaned and caught her nipple between his lips, shifting his hand to the other side. The sensation shot straight through Beth to the aching place between her thighs, and suddenly she couldn't wait another second. She shifted so she straddled his muscular legs, and rose up on her knees.

Trip moved smoothly with her, his mouth and hands never missing a beat in their delicious torment. Beth used her hand to position him, then slowly sank down, impaling herself with his hard length.

"Yesssssss." She hissed the word and held herself still, reveling in the moment. The pleasure, the incredible sense of fullness and completion, chased every other thought out of her mind. Trip's hands held her hips, guided her as she began to move. His mouth continued its onslaught on her breast, pausing only to switch to the other side.

There had been too much adrenaline in her system tonight to go slowly. She blessed Trip for letting her be in control, even while she rode him hard. He kept pace, and his taut muscles and fractured breathing attested to the fact that he was as caught up in the act as she. Sharp shards of pleasure gathered in her center, then when Trip bit down lightly with his teeth, they exploded outward. Wave after wave of pleasure spiked through her body. She felt Trip's fingers grip even tighter and his hips buck upward before his broken cry was muffled against her chest.

He held her close, their bodies still fused, as the currents of pleasure slowly subsided and reality began to swim back into focus. Big warm hands stroked gently up and down her spine, and her head tucked into his shoulder while his lips grazed her temple.

"Feel better now?" There was just a trace of humor blended with the warmth and affection in his voice. "I know I sure do."

Beth managed a rusty chuckle. "Yeah. I guess I do at that. Even better therapy than ice cream."

Trip chuckled back. "Glad to hear it." He shifted awkwardly beneath her and she looked up to see a twinge of pain flit across his face.

"I'm hurting your leg." She didn't ask; it was a simple fact. Beth lifted off of him, reluctantly breaking the connection between them. He was still mostly hard, so the slow withdrawal sent a residual thrill quivering through Beth's body.

"Trust me, it was worth a little pain." He snuggled her close to his side, both his big, strong arms protectively around her. She leaned into him, content for the moment to be coddled.

Suddenly Trip's whole body stiffened and he swore. Then he squeezed her tight. "I'm sorry, sweetheart."

"For what?" She'd almost started to doze. "My apartment?"

"Well that, too." He lifted her chin with one hand so she looked up into his eyes. His troubled, worried, eyes. "Beth, honey—we didn't—use anything. Jesus, I'm so sorry. I can't believe I didn't protect you."

She shook her head. "It's okay, Trip."

He cocked one eyebrow, and she let her gaze drop to his chest. Beth sucked in a deep breath. "I got kind of torn up when Bailey was born. Lots of scarring. It's very, very unlikely I'd ever be able to conceive again, even if the timing was right, which it isn't."

He hugged her tighter, burying his face in her hair. "Damn, Beth. I'll admit I'm relieved at the moment, but that's a crying shame. You're such a terrific mother."

She shrugged and wound her arms around his waist. Until Trip, she'd never thought she'd be in a position for it to matter. And she still wasn't, she reminded herself. Trip hadn't given a single indication of this being anything but a temporary fling.

"Time to get you clean, before you fall asleep completely." Trip stood, helping Beth to her feet as he did. He climbed out of the hot tub and guided her out as well. Instead of handing her a towel, however, he steered her to a small wooden door in the back wall of the sunroom.

Beth looked around and smiled. "Handy place for an extra bathroom." Gleaming white tile and chrome fixtures defined a simple functional bath, with a small built-in bench so you could sit and use it as a changing room. The shower was enclosed by glass block. Trip led her into it, and she was surprised at the space. Easily big enough for two, it featured jets up and down the wall as well as several in the ceiling. There was also another tile seat in here.

Trip moved to the wall and fiddled with the controls. A soft, gentle rain began, and he pulled her under the spray with him. "There were times after a work-out when I had a hard time standing long enough to get clean," he admitted. "I sure couldn't have made it upstairs, and the downstairs tub is too tiny for me. So I had this built when

I first moved in."

"Good call." She closed her eyes and turned her face up to the water, loving the feel of the warm, cleansing rain.

She heard Trip rustle about and felt him gather her hair in his hands. He added something clean-smelling, an herbal shampoo, she supposed, and began to work his hands through her smoke-scented hair. Long fingers massaged her scalp.

"If all else fails, you could make a living doing that," she murmured. It was almost hard to keep upright as he worked the fragrant lather through her hair, then rinsed it away and started over again.

His chest vibrated in a rumble as he chuckled. "Good to know." He rinsed her hair again, then worked in something else, just as yummy smelling. Conditioner, she supposed.

He left that to sit while he tended to her skin. She opened her eyes this time, to see him squirt another liquid onto a white terry wash cloth.

"Shower gel? Isn't that a little—feminine for a cowboy?" she teased. In truth it smelled like lemon and new-mown hay, not feminine at all.

His lips twitched into a smile. "My masculinity is tough enough to handle it. I like this stuff. It smells good and my skin doesn't dry out and itch. Besides..." He tapped her nose with one forefinger, then began to wash her back and shoulders with the cloth. "I keep telling you I'm not a cowboy. Haven't been for years."

"Yeah, yeah, yeah." She grinned, then dropped her head forward so he could wash the back of her neck. "And I keep telling you. Once a cowboy, always a cowboy."

"Yes, ma'am." He chuckled again, but he didn't argue. He was too busy doing marvelously decadent things to her body, she thought. If she hadn't been utterly exhausted, she'd have jumped him again, right there in the shower.

He finished washing her back, then turned her around to tenderly cleanse the front side of her. Arms first, then legs. Finally, he dropped the cloth and squirted more gel into his bare hands, then gently soaped her torso, running from her waist up to her breasts. It felt wonderful, but Beth was too tired for it to go further. Trip just smiled sweetly and washed the rest of her, pausing only briefly to caress her as he washed between her legs. After rinsing her off, he eased her down to the bench then swiftly washed himself.

A cupboard right outside the shower stall yielded fluffy white towels, and he handed her a smaller one for her hair before he wrapped her body in an enormous bath sheet. He toweled himself off with another, then wrapped it around his waist. "Ready for bed?"

Beth nodded. Trip took her hand and led the way up the stairs, turning out lights as they went. When they reached the top of the stairs, he didn't pause, just led Beth into a big room that had to be his.

A king-sized bed dominated the space, covered with a rumpled comforter in shades of green and blue. Plaid sheets in the same colors peeked out from beneath. Two small landscapes on one wall featured woods and lakes, while a portrait of Trevor graced the top of a sturdy oak dresser, along with a small television, and a handful of male sundries—watch, sunglasses, and a plastic hairbrush. A small pile of clothing had missed the wicker hamper in the corner, next to a door that was open into another bathroom.

"You can have your own room if you want," he whispered, drawing Beth into his arms. "The house has plenty. But then I'll spend the whole night standing in your doorway. After the scare you gave me tonight, I won't sleep if I can't feel you beside me."

"How do you do it, Trip?" Beth shook her head. "How do you always know exactly what to say to make me forget my better judgment?"

"I don't know. Maybe just because on some level we know each other so well?"

She snorted. "We hardly know each other at all. Not anymore."

"You're wrong, Beth. Sure, we've been apart for years, and during those years we changed. But all we did was grow up into the adults we were already well on our way to becoming. I think down deep, we both probably know each other better than we know ourselves."

Beth stifled a yawn, and Trip propelled her toward

the bathroom. "Come on, sleepyhead. I've got a new toothbrush you can use, and then you're going to bed. We'll leave the door open in case Bailey or Trevor wakes up."

She was too tired to argue. Trip disappeared while Beth brushed her teeth and used the hairdryer he'd left on the counter. The he returned, dressed in a pair of running shorts and a baggy T-shirt. He held another, similar outfit for Beth.

When she raised an eyebrow and grinned, he made a face.

"No, I don't usually sleep in pajamas, but I'd have had to get used to them pretty soon, anyway. Won't be long before Trevor is walking."

Beth went into the bedroom to dress while Trip used the bathroom. When he returned, he took the wet towels from her hands and tossed them toward the hamper in the corner. His eyes traveled up and down her body, covered in the stretchy cotton fabric.

"Those sure look better on you than they ever did on me."

Beth just shook her head and hid a grin. What on Earth was she supposed to do with him?

****

The next morning Beth and Bailey slept in, but Trevor didn't, which meant Trip didn't either. He woke to feel Beth's warm softness pressed up against his side and all he really wanted to do was hold her in his arms, but Trevor was yelling impatiently from his crib. With a whisper-light kiss on her blonde tresses, Trip climbed out of bed and trundled off to take care of Trevor before he woke Beth and Bailey.

His housekeeper wasn't due until noon, so Trip spent most of the morning guzzling down coffee and entertaining his son, trying to keep things quiet enough so Beth could sleep.

Bailey joined them about ten, rubbing her eyes and still clutching his mother's old Raggedy Ann doll. He smiled at that. Mom would be delighted to know it was bringing some comfort to another little girl.

"Mommy's still sleeping," Bailey told him, matter-of-factly. She sat down next to him on the carpet where he was playing blocks with Trevor. "I found the potty, then I found Mommy's room. She's in the biggest bed I ever saw. Do you think she got lonely in there all by herself?"

Trip swallowed a gulp of laughter. No way was he going to mention he'd shared that bed with her mother. Time to distract. "You hungry, short stuff?"

Bailey tipped her head to the side as if she had to think about the question. Then she grinned and nodded. Trip left Trevor stacking blocks and shepherded Bailey to the table.

"Frozen waffles or cereal?"

She had to think about that one too, but not for long. "Waffles, please."

Trip popped a couple of blueberry waffles into the toaster, then dug the syrup out of the fridge and put it in the microwave.

The doorbell rang while Bailey was eating. Gonzo barked and limped toward the door, tail wagging madly. Trip glanced over at Trevor, made sure he was still crawling around with his toy dump truck, then hurried to the door, hoping the commotion wouldn't wake Beth.

"Hey Harp." He gave his sister a hug as she entered the door. She didn't have any of her kids with her, which was a change of pace, and she carried two large shopping bags.

"Clothes and toiletries, as requested." She smiled at Bailey, who continued dunking waffle chunks into the puddle of syrup, then lowered her voice. "Everybody doing okay?"

"Beth's still asleep. Bailey's holding up."

"Good. Don't forget she has to go give her statement to Fitz later on. You can drop these two at my place if you want."

"Teresa should be here to watch them, but I'll let you know."

"Hello."

Beth's voice floated down from the top of the stairs. Still dressed in his T-shirt and running shorts, she descended slowly, smiling at Harper, but avoiding Trip's gaze. Since her skin flushed a bright pink as she did, he decided not to be offended.

Harper held out the shopping bags toward Beth. "I

picked up a change of clothes for each of you, and a few other necessities. Trip didn't know what size shoes you wore, so I just got flip flops. At least that way you can go into a store to get your own.

"Perfect." Beth took the bags. "I don't even know how to thank you for this."

Harper must have heard the quaver in Beth's voice. Before Trip could move to offer comfort, Harper enveloped the younger woman in a warm, motherly hug. "Just being a good neighbor. You know you'd do the same if the flip flop was on the other foot."

Both of the women chuckled at that and the mood in the room lightened perceptibly. Trip grinned at them both. "Breakfast, anyone?"

Harper shook her head. "Gotta run. I only get out without the kids for a limited time span. Talk to you both later." With a wave, she ducked out the door, leaving Trip and Beth standing their looking at each other.

****

Beth finished filling out the paperwork for her police report after what felt like hours. She glanced at her wrist before remembering she didn't have a watch at the moment and bit her lip. The clock on the wall told her she'd only been there for forty-five minutes.

"You should be able to get inside in a few days," Fitz told her. He looked so much like Trip, it would have been unsettling, except for his military-short hair and dark eyes. "The inspectors think that the structural damage is minimal. Then you'll be able to see how much can be salvaged."

Beth nodded. "A few days doesn't sound like much until you're faced with something like this. I really need my insurance paperwork as soon as possible, and I'd desperately love to know if my laptop survived." Not to mention clothes, shoes, Bailey's toys, and all the other little things that made up a person's everyday life. Things you didn't even think about until you suddenly tried to do without them.

"I'll make sure you have a copy of the police report for your insurance company. I've already been in contact with your landlord. He can't fly out right now to take care of things, but he's going to put his rental agent in charge of repairs and such. I'm sure you'll have to get together with him to sort things out."

"Yeah, I was going to stop at the real estate office after I leave here." She blotted her nose with a tissue. The cold she'd been fighting had now shown up in full force.

Fitz studied her across his wide, paper-strewn desk, then lifted an eyebrow at Trip who was just outside the office door, chatting with Fitz's secretary, a cheerful woman with silver hair. "You planning to stay at his place for the duration?"

"No. Yes." Beth shook her head in frustration. "Honestly I have no idea. I hate to be a pest. The Eliots offered to let me use the apartment above the hardware store. I haven't decided yet."

Fitz's lips twitched into what might have almost passed for a grin. "Well, I can't say that bunking with my baby brother is a picnic, but try not to kill him if you can help it." Then his expression turned stern again. "They're pretty sure it was arson, so you need to be careful. It may well be the same guy who made the phone calls. My preference would be to assign a deputy to keep an eye on you, but I don't have that kind of manpower. I'll admit, I think you're safer with Trip than you would be by yourself in another upstairs apartment."

Beth threw away the tissue then toyed with the strap of her purse. She tried to quash the little voice in her head that was doing cheers at having an excuse to stay with Trip. "But are Trip and Trevor safe if I'm there?"

Fitz's lips drew into a thin white line. "I don't know. I'm thinking that maybe the kids should stay with someone else while we look for this guy. The forensics team from the state police is going over the arson evidence. I'm hoping that we can finally get a lead on this asshole."

Bailey and Trevor stay with someone else? Beth's stomach clenched into a leaden ball at the thought of it. She didn't think Trip would go for the idea either. Not easily. Fitz seemed to sense her reluctance. "Think about it. I'm sure Harper and Jim would keep them, and she has the older girls home from school after this week to help. Meanwhile, I'll mention to the inspectors to keep an eye out for a laptop case and..." He scanned the form she'd filled out. "Your two-drawer fire-proof file cabinet. That one at least should be fine."

"Thanks." She pressed her fingers to the bridge of her nose. Damn headache just wouldn't quit.

"Oh, and before I forget, this is from Ree."

He reached around behind him and pulled a large paper shopping bag onto his desk, bearing the name of Rhiannon's shop. "She remembered how much Bailey likes stories and figured most of her books wouldn't survive the water from the fire hoses."

Beth's eyes watered up at the thoughtfulness, but Fitz wasn't done yet.

"And Shayna threw in some bottles of shampoo and stuff from the beauty shop. Plus I think there's an envelope in there from Janice at the western wear place across the street."

Now a full-fledged tear streaked down her cheek. "Damn it," she muttered, dashing it away with the back of her hand. "I *hate* being a charity case."

Fitz nodded. "Understood. But if you offend my wife by turning down the books, I'm gonna have to hurt you."

She laughed, and it felt good, even though it was crossed with a sob. "Tell Ree thank you. Bailey would rather have books than food."

"You're welcome. And don't think of it as charity. Just think of it as friends helping out friends. You'd do the same if the situations were reversed."

Trip wandered in and looked from one face to the other. "Everything okay?"

His brother nodded. "We're all set. I'll let you know when the building is clear to enter." He focused back on Beth. "And think about what I said earlier, okay? Just—think about it."

They climbed into Trip's car and headed toward the giant discount store at the edge of town. Beth refused Trip's offer to pay, and used her own credit card to buy jeans, shorts, and t-shirts for both her and Bailey. Socks, tennis shoes, and pajamas followed. Trip raised an eyebrow as she selected the last for herself.

Beth felt herself blush. She'd given up trying to convince herself that she wasn't going to be sleeping with him again. Though she had no illusions about their relationship lasting forever, she'd decided to enjoy it while it lasted. But as long as there were children in the house, she'd have pajamas on while she actually slept.

"You going to help me pick out underwear, too?" She tapped her toe on the tile floor.

He grinned. "Do I get a vote? We passed a rack with some skimpy little thongs. The peach one would look really cute—"

"Go!" She set both hands on his broad chest and pushed him toward the grocery section of the store. "Pick up a chicken and some potatoes, I'm cooking dinner."

"Fine." He leaned down and pressed a loud smack on her cheek. "Meet you at the checkout in fifteen minutes."

****

It felt really good to be wearing her own clothes again, even if they were brand new ones. And shoes. With some non-drowsy cold medicine in her system, she actually felt almost human. Beth used tongs to turn the chicken frying in the pan and chewed on her lower lip. She still hadn't talked to Trip about the idea of the kids staying somewhere else until this psycho was caught. It still didn't seem real that someone had actually tried to kill her—both her and Bailey. Someone had actually set fire to their home. Suddenly it all came crashing down on her and she dropped the tongs into the hot grease, splattering scalding droplets everywhere as the sobs racked her body.

"Beth!" Trip was there in a heartbeat, though he'd been out in the living room with the children. He flipped off the burner with one hand while his other arm gathered her close against his chest. "Honey, are you okay? Did you burn yourself?"

She pressed her face into his shirt but shook her head slightly. She might have a few pinpoint red marks on her arms, but she knew she didn't have any serious burns. He sat on a chair, drawing her down into his lap. Beth just held on tight and let all the stress and despair flow out of her in loud, gasping sobs.

"All right, sweetheart. Let it out. It's okay." His voice was a husky velvet whisper against her hair.

"Mommy?" Bailey's worried little voice came from somewhere beside her and Beth immediately tried to get herself together to soothe her daughter. But the tears just wouldn't stop.

Trip took care of it. One big hand left Beth's back and she heard him speak to the child. "Your mom's fine, honey. She's just really tired and a little upset about last night. Sometimes when scary things happen, it takes a little while, and then we cry later. Crying helps us get rid of all the bad feelings. She'll feel better after she's done."

"Oh." Bailey's tiny hand patted Beth on the back. "You can cry then, Mommy. It's okay." Then Beth heard Bailey stepping away, probably back to the living room and her pile of new books. Trip closed both arms around her then, rocking her gently on his lap until the wrenching sobs subsided into sporadic hiccoughs.

"Feel better?" Thick gentle fingers smoothed damp strands of her hair back from her face. With his other hand he tipped her chin upward so he could look at her. The tenderness and compassion shining from those clear blue eyes almost started her bawling again.

One corner of his mouth twitched into a little smile, as he handed her a paper napkin from the holder on the table. "Might want to complain to Shayna that the makeup she gave you isn't waterproof."

"Oh, lord!" Beth took the napkin and wiped her face. Shades of pink and brown and green streaked the white paper. All she'd had on was blush, a little eye shadow and mascara, but on the napkin it looked like one of Bailey's finger-paintings. She must have put the stuff on thicker than she'd thought. "I must look like an exploded clown."

Trip chuckled and kissed her nose. "Colorful, I admit. Don't know why someone as beautiful as you wears the stuff in the first place, but if it makes you feel better, be my guest." He took another napkin and blotted away a few spots she must have missed.

How did he always know exactly the right thing to say? It just wasn't—normal. He was only a human, and she needed to remember that before he broke her heart completely. Right now, though, she owed him a thank you.

"What you said to Bailey—" she began.

His smile died. "Did I say something wrong? I just didn't want her to get upset because you were crying."

"No." She placed a finger over his lips to shut him up. "It was perfect. Thank you. It's been just the two of us for so long—I'm surprised she handled it so well."

He shrugged. "I just remember what Grandma Rose—you know, Harper's mother-in-law—said to Jessie when Harp broke down after my mom died. Worked like a charm then, and it just made so much sense it kind of stuck in my head."

"Well, I'm glad it did," she admitted. She gave him one last hug, then slowly got to her feet. "I'm sorry I fell apart on you."

He shook his head. "Don't be. I expected it last night, to tell you the truth. I'm glad you finally got it out of your system. You don't have to be super-human, Beth. Look around you, sweetheart. You'll see it *isn't* just you and Bailey. You've got a lot of friends who would be there for you if you let them."

She nodded slowly. "Yeah. I think I'm finally starting to figure that out." It was why she'd brought Bailey back here in the first place—because Shirley was home. Only now she realized she'd moved back, but had held herself apart. Maybe it was time to drop those barriers she'd erected because of the damage Daniel had done to her self-esteem. She turned toward the bathroom. "I'm going to go wash my face, then I'll come see if I can salvage dinner."

"Go. Dinner will be fine."

Trip whistled and pans clattered behind her as she went. A children's show played softly on the television, while Trevor babbled at one of his toys. Somehow, all together, it sounded like—home.

Chapter Ten

Friday morning Beth's alarm went off way too early. She rolled over to swat it but ran into something warm and solid instead.

Trip!

"Ugh, is it really morning already?" His long arm snaked out from under the covers and slapped the top of his clock radio. "Are you *sure* you have to go into work today?"

Beth sat up, dragging the sheet up over her bare skin. So much for her plan to sleep in pajamas. She only vaguely remembered them coming off in the middle of the night when Trip had woken her with kisses. She did remember falling back asleep feeling more sated than she'd ever been in her life. "I do if I want to have a job on Monday."

"Surely you've got some sick leave, or personal days or something?"

Beth shook her head and stifled a yawn. Her nose was still stuffed up, but her cold seemed a bit better this morning, thank goodness. "I used it all up last winter when Bailey had the chicken pox. As it stands I'll probably be docked a day's pay for yesterday."

"Shit." Trip hauled himself up to sit beside her and slung one arm around her shoulders, tugging her up against him. "Okay. You get first dibs at the shower, and I'll go get the coffee started. But first..."

He bent his head and kissed her so thoroughly she almost forgot about work and let herself get lost in his arms again. It was Trip who eventually pulled away and rubbed his eyes with the heels of his hands.

"Okay new plan. You get in the shower and I'll go dump a tray of ice cubes down my pants. Then I'll make coffee."

He sounded so much like a cranky six-year-old she

couldn't help but laugh. "You could take a cold shower while I get Bailey up."

"Why on Earth would you wake her up? Let the poor kid sleep."

Beth shook her head. Apparently he woke up completely clueless. "I have to drop her at the sitter's on my way to work."

"Why?" Trip cocked his head. "Don't you trust her here with me?"

Jeez, he actually sounded hurt by the idea.

"I was under the impression you'd have work to do yourself," she explained, trying for the same degree of patience she'd use with Bailey. "And I want to keep her routine as close to normal as possible."

"Well this week is already not normal, so forget it. She can stay here with me and Trevor. I already talked to Teresa about it. She's fine with one extra to keep an eye on while I'm writing."

Of course he had. Beth had met his housekeeper yesterday, and she was confident that the older woman would keep things well under control. "Fine, but just for today. And no pony rides or swimming until I get home." Bailey had been fascinated last evening when Trip had taken her out to the stable and introduced her to the sturdy Shetland pony and the big Appaloosa horses. The little girl was also drawn to the tidy pond out back. After one day of chasing around an active preschooler as well as an almost-toddler, Trip would figure out his own mistake.

Trip held up three fingers in a Boy Scout salute. "Promise." Then he clambered out of bed totally unselfconscious of his nakedness and held out a hand to help Beth to her feet.

Of course she paused to look her fill on her way to the bathroom. She was only human, and despite the scars, he was a phenomenal specimen of masculinity. It didn't hurt that he stared right back, his eyes heavy-lidded and smoldering. The longer she looked, the more erect he became. She felt her own arousal blossom in response. Damn, why couldn't today have been the weekend?

"You've got about two seconds to get in the shower." His voice was a husky purr.

She couldn't resist teasing, just a little. She'd never

had this kind of opportunity to toy with a man. Daniel had pawed at her or ignored her. He'd never looked at her like he wanted to eat her for breakfast—and maybe lunch as well. "And if I don't?"

"Then you'll have to explain to Mitchell why you didn't make it to work until after noon. If then." He took one step toward her and Beth turned with a giggle and fled into the bathroom.

Trip's chuckle was warm in her ears, even through the door. "Yeah, somehow that's what I thought you'd say."

She leaned against the door for a second and just listened. There was a bit of thumping in the bedroom as he must have pulled on some clothing, then the faint tap of footsteps on the stairs, followed closely by the awkward gait she'd come to recognize as belonging to Gonzo, who'd again slept in Bailey's room. Beth was afraid Bailey would insist on taking the dog with her when they moved back into their apartment, and she hoped the separation didn't break her daughter's heart.

When she arrived at the office, dressed in a simple pair of black slacks and a pale blue knit top, one look at Donna's pinched expression told her that the day was off to an even worse start than she'd expected.

"Mr. Watkins would like to see you in his office," the older woman informed Beth coldly. "Immediately."

"Fine." Beth ducked into her cubicle to drop off her purse and ran her fingers through her hair before she squared her shoulders and marched down the hallway to her boss's big, comfortable office.

"Come in," called an impatient voice in response to her knock. She opened the door and stepped inside.

"Donna said you wanted to talk to me?" Leaving the door open, Beth approached the wide oak desk. Mitchell's pale forehead wrinkled beneath his shiny bald head as he peered at her, his watery blue eyes narrowed. A navy suit jacket was open over a white dress shirt that strained at the buttons over his bulging gut.

"Sit."

Beth sat and folded her hands in her lap. Mitchell expected his employees to maintain a ladylike demeanor at all times. "What can I do for you, Mitchell?"

He frowned. "The sheriff's department called yesterday. Said there'd been a fire at your apartment."

Beth nodded. "That's right."

He fiddled with a pen, clicking the button repeatedly. "You all right?"

Beth had to fight not to show how shocked she was at this evidence of human concern. It was one thing she hadn't expected from him. She nodded slowly. "Aside from a head cold, Bailey and I are both fine."

Mitchell gave one crisp nod. "Good." He played with the pen some more. An expression of acute distaste crossed his visage. "Donna seems to think you're shacking up with your boyfriend or something. Apparently the whole town's talking about it."

Beth felt all the blood drain from her face. So that's what this was about. Mitchell and Donna were both ultra-conservative. Since up until now Beth hadn't had a personal life to speak of, it had never been a problem. A sharp pain took up residence in her left temple. Of course the entire town knew where she'd spent the last two nights. Small towns were great for some things, but the gossip around here flew faster than leaves in the October wind.

"I heard the Eliots offered you use of the apartment above the hardware store. Don't you think that might be a little more—discreet?" Now the pen tapped rhythmically on his leather desk blotter.

Beth opened her mouth, then closed it again. How to tell him that the sheriff thought she was safer with Trip? She really didn't want to discuss the whole stalker thing with her boss. She was sure he'd somehow work it out to be all her fault.

"Thing is, this company has a certain reputation to maintain," Mitchell continued.Of course it did. And that reputation probably mattered far more to Mitchell than the well being of one measly accountant.

Beth just gave another hopeless nod.

"And while I know that you young people do things a little differently today, it just doesn't look right, you flat out living with a man."

Tap-tap-tap. The pen picked up speed until Beth was afraid it was going to wriggle right out of his hand and onto the carpet.

"But..." Even she didn't know what she was going to say.

Mitchell held up a hand to stop her.

"I mean it's not like you're even engaged, or anything. We could all understand it then."

Engaged? Yeah right. That was soooo not going to happen.

"Of course any respectable young man would open his home to his fiancée and her child in this kind of situation..."

The facts slid into place in her brain with an almost audible click. Mitchell was giving her an out. He wasn't going to fire her. Yet. She squeezed her eyes shut and prayed that Trip would forgive her for the whopper she was about to tell.

"Of course we're engaged."

The pen stopped. Mitchell gaped, then almost instantly recovered his composure. "You are?"

She blinked rapidly then nodded, fishing in her pocket for a tissue. Darned runny nose!

"Well why didn't you say so?"

Okay, time to lie through her teeth. "We weren't in a hurry, you know? Planned to take it slowly, make sure it was going to work out, since we both have children and everything. Then maybe announce it later this summer."

Apparently it had been the right thing to say. "Oh, of course. Well, congratulations, my dear. I'm sure you'll be very happy together. We'll be sorry to lose you here of course..."

"Huh?" This time her jaw did drop. "Why?"

"Why what?" Mitchell tilted his head to the side and peered at her.

"Why would you lose me here? I'm engaged, not dying."

"You were planning to stay? After the wedding? I'd just assumed... I mean you're both young... Surely there'll be more children..."

Okay, time to nip that line of thinking in the bud. "I'm not going to quit, Mitchell. We're not planning any more children at this point, and even if we did, lots of women work and have babies these days." Not for

Mitchell Watkins they didn't.

"Oh. Of course." He straightened a stack of papers on his desk in a gesture she recognized as dismissal. Then he looked up at her again. "Are you sure you're all right? You look kind of—pale. Maybe you should take the rest of today off, just in case."

Really? The old coot was willing to give her a second day off? Beth would have looked for the catch, but since the pounding in her temple was accelerating, she was inclined to agree. "If you don't mind," she sighed. "That would be great. This cold is a beast and I haven't exactly been sleeping well since the fire." Which was entirely true, though not exactly for the reasons she hoped he'd assume.

"Understandable, of course." He straightened his papers again and nodded crisply. "Then it's settled. See you bright and early Monday morning. And send Donna in on your way out."

Beth thanked him again, then did as she was told. Donna looked none too happy about either the summons or the idea that Beth was leaving again. Before she could make it safely out the door, though, Fitz Hall strode in—carrying Beth's laptop case. It was dirty, but looked amazingly intact.

"Oh!" She ran over to Fitz, almost hugged him without thinking about it. "You found it?"

His lips twitched in that way she'd figured out was a suppressed smile. "Well, the arson inspectors found it. Said it looks to be fine. The vinyl case shook off most of the water."

That did it. She did hug him. Sidearm and all, right there in the middle of the reception area, with a couple of customers watching. Was this what it was like to have family? The thought brought tears to her eyes. "Thank you, thank you, thank you."

"You're welcome." He disengaged himself and handed it over. "Your file cabinet is in my office, along with a couple of plastic storage tubs. Want me to have someone put it in your car? And there's a garbage bag with some clothes and toys in it. One of the firemen has a kid—said he figured Bailey would want a few of her own things around. They'll all need to be laundered—probably more than once."

Tears started leaking from the corners of Beth's eyes. This time Fitz put his hand on her shoulder and patted it awkwardly. "Hey now. Everything's gonna be fine."

Beth forced herself to smile up at him. If he only knew. By this time tomorrow half the town would have heard about her so-called engagement, and then he'd probably come after her with his gun. She sniffled and nodded. "Tell the firemen thanks, okay? And I'm heading home—I mean, I'm leaving now. I can put the stuff in my car."

She drove back to Trip's with a load of belongings in the back of her car, and an even heavier load on her mind.

****

Trip was in the downstairs bedroom he used as an office when he heard a car pulling into his drive. Beth had left an hour or so ago, and Teresa was already here watching the kids, so he had no idea who it could be.

He was at the front door looking out when he recognized the car. His stomach clenched into a ball of panic. What was Beth doing home so early? Had something happened? He was out the door and down the drive before she'd turned off the engine.

"Are you all right?" He opened her door and asked even as she was getting out of the driver's seat.

"Yes, of course," she assured him, but her voice trembled and so did her hand. "The firemen rescued some things from my apartment."

He saw the heavy metal file cabinet, the plastic bins, and the two large garbage bags in the back end of the wagon. He'd have to wait for help to haul the cabinet into the house, but at least Beth would know her things were safe. "Mitchell didn't have a problem with you leaving?"

She sighed and slumped against the side of the car. "He gave me one more day off. I think he was afraid I was going to pass out on the office floor. Aside from this stupid virus, the headache I had all day yesterday came back with a vengeance the minute I set foot in the office."

Trip put both hands on her shoulders and studied her face. She did look pale, damn it. "Maybe we should get you to a doctor," he suggested.

"No." Beth shook her head with enough vehemence to

convince him she meant it. "It's just a cold and stress—nothing a nap or a soak in your hot tub won't cure. But..." She squeezed her eyes shut. "There is something else. Something I need to talk to you about. And if you want me to leave after I tell you, I'll understand."

"Leave? Sweetheart, you're not making any sense. Let's get you upstairs for a nap. We can talk once you're feeling better." He took her arm and propelled her up the steps and into the house.

She looked around the living room once they were inside. "Where are the children? And isn't that Teresa's car outside?"

"She's upstairs doing something. I imagine Bailey is watching her every move and Trevor is playing in his room." He listened closely and sure enough, he heard footsteps and the sound of Teresa's patient voice as she answered one of Bailey's never-ending questions.

"Good." Beth sank down into one of the leather club chairs and gestured to the one next to it. "Sit. Please."

He did, then leaned over and took both of her chilly hands in his. "What happened, Beth? Did somebody in town give you trouble? Your boss..."

"Stop." She squeezed down on his hands. "Listen for a minute, okay."

Heart thudding in his chest, he nodded. "Okay."

"First of all, the entire town appears to know I'm staying here."

That didn't bother him a bit. Hell, he felt like beating his chest and shouting it from the rooftops. But he kept his mouth shut and nodded at her to keep going.

"My boss was less than pleased. You do remember that some of the people in this town are very conservative, don't you?"

"A few are downright archaic, but not many."

She looked at him with such a stern expression he had to suppress a smile. It vanished almost immediately as he figured out that Watkins was one of the puritanical ones and was giving Beth trouble about being here with Trip.

"What did he say?" He'd take the man apart with his bare hands if he had to.

"Not too much." Beth pulled her hands away from

Trip's and started twisting them together in her lap. "It's just...he said...and I kind of...well..."

Trip bit his lip to keep a laugh from surfacing. "Honey, is my brother going to be calling and asking you where you hid your boss's body?"

Finally she smiled, and Trip allowed himself to breathe again. If Beth was smiling, the world couldn't have crashed and burned around them.

"No," she admitted. "But he might hear something else."

"Oh?" He smiled back. "Come on, spit it out."

She took a deep breath and closed her eyes. "I told Mitchell we were engaged."

Surely that little bitty lie wasn't what had her so tense. There had to be more. "And?"

She opened her eyes and looked at him. "I told my boss that you and I were engaged—as in about to be married. I'm sorry. But he was making noises about my behavior being inappropriate, and I was afraid he was going to fire me, and..."

"Stop." Trip laid a finger over her lips to stop her babbling. "That's it? Mitchell was giving you crap about staying here and you told him it was okay because we're engaged?"

She nodded glumly. When he removed his finger she added. "I'm sorry. I know it was a stupid thing to do. If you want me to get a motel room, I'll understand."

"Idiot." He shook his head. Then he took hold of her arms and tugged, until she was forced to leave her chair and land in his lap. "Why should I mind? All that means is I get to do this—" He bent his head and kissed her until her lips softened and started kissing him back. Then he pulled away just an inch or so. "Openly and in public." And maybe, he thought, it would deter her stalker if he thought she was spoken for. Or at least shake up the bastard enough to make him show his hand so Fitz could nail him.

"Trip—"

She sounded like she was about to object, so he kissed her again, and didn't stop until he heard Bailey yell, "Mommy!" and start clattering down the stairs.

****

The rest of the afternoon was spent laundering stuffed animals, including the oversized Señor Bear, who was a challenge to fit in the washer. Trip and Teresa somehow managed it while Beth took a nap. Later came Bailey's first riding lesson on Frodo the pony. Beth watched with her heart in her throat as Trip tenderly lifted Bailey into the saddle then walked alongside her around the small paddock adjoining the stable.

"He's a good kid," said Teresa Ryan from somewhere behind Beth. Beth turned to find the older woman holding Trevor who must have just woken from his nap. He'd been sleeping when they'd left the house.

"Trevor? He's a great kid." Beth automatically reached out to take him from the other woman's arms.

Teresa handed him over, and he was still sleepy enough to cuddle down into Beth's shoulder. "Him too." She looked out at the paddock. "But I meant his dad. He's been through a lot in the last year."

Beth nodded. "I know." So that's where this was going. She'd expected to be warned off by Fitz, or maybe Harper, but she supposed Teresa had more or less adopted Trip, so she had the right.

"He could use someone to be there for him. He's not nearly as tough as he tries to pretend."

Beth knew that too. But what did she have to offer? Their relationship had been all about him taking care of her so far. He deserved so much more.

"Anyway," Teresa wiped her hands on the dishtowel tucked into the waistband of her jeans. "The potato salad and coleslaw are all set for the big shindig tomorrow. Steaks and hotdogs are in the fridge and the ice cream is in the freezer. Anything else you need before I go?"

Shindig? Tomorrow? Beth just stood and stared.

Teresa chuckled. "I'll take that as a no." She chucked Trevor on the chin then turned toward the driveway. "See you Monday morning."

"What has your daddy gotten us into this time?" Beth asked Trevor, who was apparently dozing in her arms. It felt so nice to have a baby to snuggle that she didn't want to disturb him, so she simply sat down on a bale of hay and watched Trip walk the pony around the yard. Tonight. They definitely had to talk. Tonight.

****

They cleared up most of her questions over dinner. Trip was relieved that she didn't seem to mind about the barbecue tomorrow. He hadn't meant to blindside her, but they'd both forgotten about the weekend completely after the fire. The only reason he'd remembered it at all was that Teresa had reminded him when she arrived this morning. When he'd invited Beth to his pond-opening party, he'd meant to tell her the rest of his family was coming, but somehow when he was talking to Beth his brain never seemed to be working full-speed. She took it remarkably well when she discovered they'd have nine extra adults and half a dozen kids showing up the next afternoon. In fact, all she did was ask to invite Shayna as well, to which Trip readily agreed.

"Well, they all knew I was here with you anyway," she sighed. "Might as well get it all out in the open right from the start."

Yeah, that's exactly what they needed to talk about now, he thought. The dishes were done, both kids were in bed, and they were sitting in the living room working on their respective laptops.

Trip darted upstairs and got a small pouch out of the safe in his bedroom closet. Beth barely looked up when he returned, she was so intent on whatever website design element she was working on. Trip coughed loudly as he shut down his own computer.

No response. He cleared his throat. Nothing.

He leaned close and murmured her name. "Beth?"

She jumped a little and looked up, blinking. "What?"

"Do you need to get more work done tonight, or can I talk to you for a few minutes?"

"Oh!" Her eyes flew wide. "Sure." She typed a few swift keystrokes, then folded the laptop closed. "What's up?"

He pulled the velvet pouch out of the back pocket of his jeans. "I thought you should have this on when everybody shows up tomorrow." Opening the pouch he withdrew a ring. A large pearl flanked by two tiny diamonds nestled in an antique gold setting. "My grandmother's," he explained. "I guess it sort of came with the house."

Actually it had come to him because CJ had their mother's and Fitz had inherited Grandmother Hall's. So Grandma Ryan's had been earmarked for Trip's bride. It was the least valuable of the three, but the glowing pearl and warm gold band would be gorgeous against Beth's honey-toned skin.

"No way!" She scooted back away from him like he was holding out a snake. Trip tried not to let himself be hurt by her horrified reaction, but it didn't quite work.

"Look. They're going to expect it." He set the ring down on the coffee table. "If you want people to believe we're engaged, you're going to need a ring. If you don't like this one, I can go buy a diamond."

"It's only for a couple weeks," she argued. "Just until I can get back into my apartment. And I'd assumed we'd tell your family the truth."

"Fine." He shrugged, wishing he really didn't care. "Your boss will know the truth by Tuesday, but if that's the way you want to play it, it's up to you."

"You're saying your family can't keep a secret?" He heard the almost-laugh that bubbled in her throat. Poor Beth had a long way to go before she understood the complexity of a family the size of his.

"Any one of the adults, I'd trust with the deepest darkest secrets of my soul. But the whole lot of them together? Hopeless. One would say something to another, and odds are one of the kids would hear. And they'd mention it to a friend, who would tell a parent. Eventually it would be all over town. And what about Bailey? What are we going to tell her? She's so damn smart, she's going to figure out that something's going on. And she talks to the kids at the sitter's and they talk to their parents…"

"You're right." Beth crossed her legs in the chair and rested her elbows on her knees, her chin on her hands. "It was a dumb idea. This is never going to work."

"It's not as simple as it could be," he agreed. "But it isn't impossible." How did he admit that he'd be humiliated if she told her boss she'd lied? Or if they "broke up" before the engagement had ever really begun.

"You think there's a way to make it work?"

He nodded. "One that's so simple it's foolproof." His gut clenched into a ball of cement.

"And that is…?" She looked like she was holding her breath, waiting for his explanation. The steady thrum of arousal that was always there between them added another layer of tension to an already nerve-wracking conversation.

"We get engaged."

Now it was him holding his breath, waiting for her response.

"You mean we pretend." She licked her lips. "To everyone."

He shook his head. "No. I mean we get engaged. For real."

"But—"

"Jesus, I know I'm screwing this up, Beth. I'm great with words, on paper, but when it really matters, I never manage to get it right." He scrubbed both hands over his face and took a deep breath, let it out slowly. "Look. We've got something going between us. Something deeper, more important than anything I've ever felt before. I think you feel it too. Having you here these last few days—it feels right. It feels like home. I don't want to lose that, Beth. I've made a lot of mistakes in my life, and I don't want to add losing you to the list."

"But marriage—I'm not sure I'm ready for that, Trip. I'm not sure I ever will be again. I went down that road once, and it was awful. I can't just jump into it again. I have Bailey to think about…" Her face was pale, her eyes wide and panicked.

"I know." He forced the words past the lump in his throat. Needing desperately to touch her, he reached out and laid his hands on her forearms. "That's why I said get engaged, not get married. I know that's a step you're not ready for yet. But the truth is, I love you Beth. And I love Bailey. Neither of those things is going to change. I want both of you in my life. And if a long engagement is the most comfortable way for you to make that happen, then that's what I'll take."

So many emotions flooded Beth's brain at once that she couldn't sort out just one to work with. Trip was proposing *marriage*? To her? Or if not marriage, then at least something so close there was no real separation of the concepts.

He'd said he loved her.

Her!

She wasn't sure of much right now, but she'd swear on her soul that she'd just heard Trip Hall say that he was in love with her—Elizabeth Corcoran, a.k.a. Lizzie the Nerd MacArthur.

This *so* could not be happening!

And yet...

She looked into Trip's cornflower blue eyes and saw every dream she'd ever dreamt. He meant it, she could see that. He might have always been a flirt and a charmer, but he'd never been a liar. Whether the sentiment would last past the heat of the moment was another issue, but right here, right now, he meant every word he said. Beth's heart melted.

She picked up the ring off the table and turned it around and around in her fingers. It was the most beautiful piece of jewelry she'd ever seen. She vaguely remembered it on Mrs. Ryan's hand. Trip's grandparents had been in love until the day they died. A couple could do a lot worse than to borrow a little of their karma when starting out in a new relationship.

But was it fair to agree when she just wasn't sure? Was it fair to Trip? To herself? To their children?

"Just give it a chance, Beth. Give *us* a chance." His coaxing tone was sweet and seductive. Her whole body responded, heating and softening as it always seemed to for Trip. She had to force herself to concentrate on her thoughts, instead of just giving in to her physical and emotional desire to please him.

Think, Beth! When Daniel had died, she promised herself she'd never let her emotions get the best of her judgment again. She'd never trust a handsome charmer with her heart or her daughter's well-being. But Trip *wasn't* Daniel. He'd been a better father to Bailey already than Daniel had ever been.

"I promise. No pressure. We take it at whatever pace you want."

Trip's shoulders had tightened, as had the tendons in his throat. Whether he wanted to admit it or not, he was nervous, and she knew if she said no, he'd be hurt. Really, honestly hurt. And she just didn't have it in her to hurt him. Not when he'd done so much for her, not when she'd loved him all her life. She smiled and held the ring out toward him.

"So it's a no, then." He sighed and took it from her hand. "It's okay. I never wanted to pressure you, Beth. I'm sorry."

"No." She unfolded her legs, and looked up at him, then held out her left hand, fingers splayed. "I mean yes. You put it on. That's how this is supposed to work, isn't it?"

"You mean..." Surprise, and she thought, hope flashed across his face.

Beth nodded. "I would love to be your fiancée, Trip. I can't promise more. I'd like to, but...not yet. If you can live with that, then my answer is yes."

"I can live with that." His voice was deep, husky as if his throat was clogged.

He took her hand with his left one, then used his right to slide the ring onto her finger. It stuck at the knuckle, and Trip winced. "Sorry. I didn't even stop to think that it might not fit."

"It fits fine." Beth wiggled the ring past her knuckle to where it belonged. "You wouldn't want it to come off too easily, now would you?"

"Guess not." He lifted her hand to his lips and kissed the finger that held his ring. "Looks like it belongs there, doesn't it?"

"Yeah." Beth smiled up at him through a faint haze of tears. "Yeah it does."

Chapter Eleven

The big announcement the next day went about as Trip had expected. As the only two in town, Fitz and Ree had, in fact, heard the rumor already, but that didn't detract from the general excitement and the avalanche of well-wishes. So had Shayna and Rick Anderson, who had been invited at the last minute. And if one of the other of his brothers occasionally cast Trip a slightly skeptical glance from under one raised eyebrow, it was nothing that Trip couldn't ignore. In his mind the engagement was real, and he was damn sure going to enjoy it. His body still tingled from the private celebration he and Beth had indulged in the night before. He looked over to where she waded in the pond with Bailey, wearing matching orange swimsuits with yellow and white daisies, and it was all he could do not to drag her back into the bedroom and celebrate all over again.

"Come on, I'll help you get the food on the grill." CJ spoke from behind Trip's shoulder. "Before my wife starts chewing on the picnic table."

Trip looked over to where Allison was munching on chips and dip with a blissful expression on her face, and laughed. His sister-in-law seemed to be enjoying every minute of her pregnancy. "Well, she's entitled, I guess." He stood and started toward the house.

"Yeah." CJ made a face. "Easy to say when you're not the one who has to go find ice cream at two in the morning."

"Poor baby." Trip clapped his oldest brother on the back. "Sucks to be you, doesn't it?" Trip knew perfectly well that CJ had never been happier in his life.

CJ growled and gave Trip a mock shove. "Just wait. You'll have your turn soon enough. We'll see who's whining then."

"No." Even Trip heard the hint of wistfulness in his

own voice. Forcing it down, he strode swiftly down the hallway to the kitchen. "We're done with two."

"Ah. That's cool." CJ started hefting bowls and platters.

Trip watched his brother carefully, wondering where CJ was going with this.

"Bailey's a keeper, that's for sure." Apparently CJ had decided to let the matter drop. "And between them, she and Trevor are sure to be a handful. You did good, little brother. Took you long enough, but you did good."

Trip grunted, grabbed up the platter loaded with steaks and hot-dogs, along with some veggie burgers for Ree. He held a bottle of barbecue sauce with two fingers under the platter. "Yeah, I think so, too."

He'd turned to follow CJ back to the yard when he heard the doorbell. Who was showing up now? He wondered if maybe one of the kids had run around to the front of the house as a joke. Since his hands were full, he yelled, "Come in," as he moved toward the door.

A total stranger stepped inside. "Howard Hall?" A stranger wearing desert camouflage military fatigues.

No. As he stood there blinking, Trip recognized the face. His knees went weak and he almost dropped the meat. He did drop the plastic bottle of barbecue sauce. He lowered the platter to the kitchen table with a loud thunk. At least it wasn't a crash.

"I'm Trip." He stepped toward the other man and extended his hand politely. "You're Drew. Andrew Lawson. Your sister spoke about you a lot. Kept your photo on her mantel." Lori Lawson had been Lorelei's real name—she'd used Lorelei LaBelle professionally. Tall and rugged, with short-cropped light brown hair, Drew Lawson resembled Lorelei physically, but not at all in demeanor. He shook Trip's hand with a firm, almost aggressive grip. His gray eyes darted around the house. Trip had no doubt that he noted every detail, and was busily filing away every fact.

"Looks like I'm interrupting a party," Lawson offered with stiff politeness. "Did I catch you at a bad time?"

Like you didn't intend to catch me off-guard, Trip thought. "Just a family gathering," he said out loud. "Please join us. There's plenty of food. I'm sure you're here to visit your nephew."

The other man nodded. "That was my plan, yes. I've just finished up with Lori's attorneys in California and visited her grave. Thought I'd stop and introduce myself before I head back to Texas."

"I'm sorry about your sister," Trip said honestly. "Things might not have gone all that well between us at the end, but I am sorry that she's dead."

Lawson nodded. "I read the transcripts of the custody hearing. I know she walked out while you were in a coma."

Trip nodded. What did the man want? Was he just here to visit Trevor? Or was he going to challenge Trip for custody? Lorelei's boyfriend at the time of her death had been a Hollywood sycophant, who hadn't wanted Trevor, not enough to really put up a fight. This man was different. Drew Lawson was a warrior, who must just recently have been rotated back to the US from the Middle East. Trip hoped he wasn't going to have another custody battle on his hands.

"Well, Trevor's out back, with his cousins." Trip picked up the platter and jabbed an elbow at the fridge. "Grab yourself a beer or a soda, and come on outside. You may as well meet the whole gang since you're here."

With a thin smile, Lawson opened the refrigerator and helped himself to a cold beer. As the two men started down the hall to the back door, it sprang open, and a smiling Beth stepped inside, Trevor in her arms. She'd wrapped a beach towel around her waist but was still damp and lovely in her swimming suit, and Trip felt his heart clench.

"Wondered where you'd gotten off too," she called to Trip. "This guy needs changing, but the horde is getting restless and demanding meat." She smiled at the new arrival, and shifted Trevor to her left hip, so she could hold out her right hand. "Hi, I'm Beth."

"Major Andrew Lawson," the officer replied. He shook her hand. "Pleasure to meet you, ma'am."

"Are you a friend of Trip's?" she asked. "From California, maybe? I know you didn't grow up around here."

"No ma'am. I'm from Texas, originally. Spent the last

few years everywhere but." His keen gaze was fixed on Trevor, and Trip knew what he had to do.

Trip cleared his throat. "Major Lawson, this is my fiancée, Beth Corcoran, and yes, that's Trevor. Beth, this is Drew Lawson—Trevor's uncle."

Beth's eyes flew wide and she instinctively gathered Trevor closer in her arms. Drew's lifted eyebrows registered surprise at the word fiancée, but he didn't change his stance or his well-mannered smile.

Trip wanted to take Beth and their kids and hide, but he knew that was stupid. Even if Lawson was here to try to claim Trevor, he didn't have a leg to stand on legally or morally. Acting weird and paranoid would only give the man grounds where he really had none.

Right then Trevor decided to fuss. Trip couldn't take him as he had nowhere to put the tray of meat, so he sent Beth a pleading look. "Can you go ahead and change him, then bring him back outside? I should get the steaks and hot dogs on the grill before the natives revolt."

"S-s-sure." Beth nodded. He imagined she was relieved to have a moment away from facing the crowd, as well as the new arrival. She darted into the downstairs bathroom and shut the door behind her.

"Pretty woman," Lawson noted as they continued toward the door. "Known her long?"

Trip chuckled, though it was a little forced. Was Lawson trying to determine if Trip had been involved with Beth and Lorelei at the same time? He'd better not be making any nasty assumptions about Beth. "Since first grade. But we just reconnected since I moved home last winter."

Then they were outside and a dozen pairs of curious eyes were turned their way. "Shit." Lawson sipped his beer and murmured under his breath. "When you said family get-together, you really meant it, didn't you?"

Trip knew Lorelei and her brother had been raised pretty much alone, with no other siblings or even cousins nearby. He gave the other man a wry grin. "Yep. You want them in order of age or viciousness?"

Harper was already bearing down on them with all the subtlety of a steamship, so Lawson didn't really have much choice. He raised one eyebrow at Trip. "So which one's your attorney? And which one's the cop?"

****

Beth felt like she'd been punched in the stomach. Trevor's *uncle*? Where the hell had he come from? Besides Texas. What was he doing here? Judging by Trip's worried expression, this wasn't a friendly family visit. Beth knew very little about the woman who had been Trevor's mother, but what she did know, she didn't like. She knew Lorelei had abandoned Trip when he was hurt, that she hadn't told Trip about his son, and that she'd been driving while drunk—with Trevor in the car. Given half a chance, Beth would have cheerfully strangled the woman herself.

She finished changing Trevor and rejoined the party, forcing a pleasant smile on her face. The tone of the gathering had grown considerably colder during the short time she'd been inside.

"What's he doing here?" Shayna asked, slipping up beside Beth and holding out a cold can of diet soda.

"I have no idea." She set Trevor down on the grass beside several of his toys and took the soda, popping the top and gulping down a good bit of the cold liquid. Her eyes had already found Bailey, who was busy building a sand castle with Trip's nieces and Shayna's daughter by the edge of the pond. Since teen-aged Jessica was between the little ones and the water's edge, Beth turned her attention back to Shayna.

"He's decorative, that's for sure. Definitely something about a man in uniform. I love seeing Rick in his National Guard gear, even though I'm terrified he'll be called up one of these days." Shayna plopped down in a lawn chair near Trevor and patted the one beside it.

"Hmmm." Beth sat, and took a moment to be glad that Trip was no longer attached to the Marines. She'd seen pictures of him in uniform, though, and had to admit, he'd looked awfully good.

About then the uniformed man strode over and introduced himself to Shayna. Then he turned to Beth. "I understand congratulations are in order. I hope you can forgive me for accidentally crashing your engagement party."

"As long as you're here for a friendly visit, you're

more than welcome," Beth replied. "I can certainly understand wanting to meet your nephew."

"Uh-oh. Looks like Kenny and Mike got into the watermelon. Better go clean them up before the whole place gets sticky." Shayna was out of her chair and moving even as she spoke.

"May I?" Major Lawson gestured at the chair Shayna had just vacated.

Beth nodded, and he sat down beside her, his gaze on the little boy playing at his feet. Gonzo had wandered over and settled in beside Trevor, and was watching the stranger with canine suspicion.

"I gather that the little girl in the orange swimsuit is your daughter," the major noted. "She's a cutie. She's what, four or five?"

"Almost four," Beth told him. "But she sometimes seems older."

"And her father…?"

"Died shortly after she was born."

"Sorry." His expression was thoughtful, but Beth thought she saw some real grief behind the gray eyes.

"And I'm sorry about your sister. I never met her, but I'm sure she was a lovely person."

He smiled weakly. "She was when she was younger. Prettiest thing you ever saw, bright and funny. But she'd changed somewhere along the way. She kept diaries, you know. I read them last week. I'd have never recognized them by the tone. Something about the life she chose turned her hard, superficial. More than a little greedy."

"And you needed to make sure that the man she'd been with wasn't the same," Beth intuited.

The major nodded.

"He's not." Beth watched Trevor tug on Gonzo's fur, pulling himself up into a standing position. The poor dog just sighed and held still, accepting the abuse. Trevor crowed and leaned toward Beth. Then with a happy chortle, the child let go of Gonzo and took a wobbly step toward Beth.

"Trip!" Beth ignored what the soldier was saying as she held out her hands to Trevor, who was still a few feet away. "Trip, Trevor is walking."

"I see him." She heard Trip's uneven gait as he

limped over from the barbecue. The others gathered around, cheering Trevor on. There was a soft click, so Beth knew someone had gotten these precious first steps on film. Right before Trevor reached Beth, he stumbled, falling the last few inches into her outstretched hands. Beth scooped up Trevor, and was engulfed in return by Trip's arms as he gathered them both into his embrace.

"Way to go, big guy!" Trip pressed a smacking kiss his son's head.

The laughing throng of relatives dispersed. Beth handed Trevor into Trip's arms and smiled at them both. Trip moved away, chatting with CJ who had taken over at the grill. Beth turned to see the major still sitting next to her with an odd look on his face as he watched Trip and Trevor. Impulsively, she reached over and patted his hand. "They can be overwhelming, can't they? I'm an only child, so I constantly feel like I've fallen down a rabbit hole. But they're all good people—the best. Any one of them would lay down their life for any of the others. And that includes Trevor. So you'll never need to worry. With all those cousins watching out for him, he'll be lucky to get away with anything, his whole life."

"I'm beginning to see that," the major admitted. He drained the last drops from his can of beer. "But I want to know my nephew. You think they'll have a problem with that?"

She shook her head. "I think they'd find it odd if you didn't. Speaking as Trevor's future stepmother, I can tell you that you're welcome to visit any time." The minute she's sensed a threat to Trip and Trevor, she'd given up pretending even to herself that she wasn't going to marry Trip. Maybe not tomorrow, but she wasn't about to let go of her claim on either one of them.

"Thank you." He held out his hand and shook hers. "And now I think it's time for me to go. Tell Hall I'll be in touch tomorrow. We can set up a time for me to stop by."

Beth watched him go, wondering once again just what she'd gotten herself into.

****

Beth took Bailey to dinner at the Andersons' the following night, leaving Trip and Trevor on their own as they met Drew Lawson at Benedetto's. Lorelei's brother had suggested that they get together on neutral ground. Figuring that would be easier on everybody, Trip had agreed. So here they sat, eyeing one another across the table like a pair of old West gunfighters.

"I'm heading for Texas first thing in the morning," the other man said after they'd placed their orders. "I'd like to come up again in a month or two, maybe for a weekend, once I get things settled on the ranch."

"Anytime," Trip replied. "You're family to Trevor, which means you're family to me. You'll always be welcome."

Lawson nodded thoughtfully. "I appreciate that. I don't know what I expected to find here, but it wasn't to discover that everything is so—settled. That's more than I could offer him, at first at least. All those brothers and sisters of yours—not to mention your fiancée—you're a lucky man, Hall. I've got no problem with my nephew being raised in the middle of that."

Trip grunted. "Glad to hear it." Mentally he breathed a huge sigh of relief to know that Lawson wasn't going to make a mess of things.

"Lori kept diaries. Did you know that?"

Trip shook his head, his shoulders automatically bracing for a blow.

"She'd changed, somewhere along the way. I'll always remember her as a smart, sweet little kid, but that probably wasn't the woman you knew."

Trip tipped his hand back and forth. "She had her moments."

"Did you know she'd planned to have an abortion?"

Trip sucked in a breath and shook his head. After a few tries, he managed to speak. "I was kind of surprised she hadn't."

"Turned out there was a movie role she was up for. The character was pregnant. She thought she'd have a better chance of getting the part if she really was."

All Trip could think was thank god for that movie! He swallowed the lump in his throat.

"After, she figured she could get some cash out of your family—but then you started to recover and she chickened out."

Was he supposed to thank the man for telling him

this? Trip supposed it was good to finally know what had happened, but the very possibility that Trevor might not have happened made him sick to his stomach.

"Anyway, here's some information I put together for you." Lawson lifted a manila folder from the seat beside him and handed it across the table to Trip. "Family trees, medical histories, that sort of thing. The ranch was left to me outright, but Lori did get some property. It'll be administered by a trust for Trevor, in case he wants it some day. There'll be money, too, for his education."

Trip waved a hand. He'd known Trevor had some inheritance from his mother that the lawyers were still hashing out. He hadn't expected it to be much. Lorelei had gone through money like it was water. "That won't be necessary, but it's good to know you'll be keeping an eye on it for him. I may be technically unemployed, but I'm not short on funds."

Lawson grinned. "I know. I had the lawyers check."

Trip forced down his instinctive indignation and sighed. "Hell, I'd have done the same thing."

"Figured." Lawson sipped at an iced tea, then gestured at the folder again. "My contact info is all in there too. Cell number, the ranch address, all of that. Plus the family attorney and the ranch foreman, just in case. Trevor's my beneficiary with Uncle Sam. I'm supposed to get my official discharge any day now, but you never know. Shit happens, and I could be recalled at any time."

Trip hadn't expected to like the man, but he did, despite the awkward circumstances. There was one more topic he needed to broach, and it was another tough one. He waited until they'd been served, and Trevor was chewing on a teething biscuit.

"You know I'm planning to get married soon," he began, pushing around a forkful of Ruthanne's lasagna.

"Uh-huh. I liked her, just in case you were wondering." Lawson scooped up a mouthful of mashed potatoes and chicken gravy. "Oh, God this is good. I've been eating Army food for way too long."

"Beth and I haven't discussed it yet, but I'd like to adopt her daughter Bailey. There's no family there, and it worries me that if, God forbid, something should happen to Beth, I might not be able to get custody. I'd have never thought about that a year ago, but now, it's pretty much on my mind if you understand what I mean."

"Understood." Lawson chewed on his fried chicken while Trip ate his lasagna. "I think I see where you're going with this. You want her to adopt Trevor as well."

Trip nodded. "I don't mean it as any sort of insult to your sister—not really, not even now. But she's gone. And Beth's a great mother. Besides, this way Trev and Bailey could really grow up as brother and sister, with no weird step-anythings to worry about."

"I see." The other man chewed silently. "I can understand that, I guess." There was a long pause, then he nodded slowly. "How about if I have my lawyer draw up an agreement? I won't contest an adoption, as long as I'm guaranteed visitation rights."

Trip weighed the words then held out his hand. "Agreed."

They shook, then Lawson's lips quirked into a trace of a grin. "So when's the wedding?"

Trip laughed. It was a little forced, but it was still a laugh, and it dissipated most of the tension that had hovered over the table. "Not sure yet. Hopefully soon. Very, very soon."

****

Beth strapped Bailey into her car seat while Shayna stood beside the car holding half a pie in a foil-covered pan.

"You really don't need to send pie home with me, Shay. Trip and I are both perfectly competent adults. We can make our own food." Once Bailey was settled, Beth gave Shayna a hug.

"I know, but I was in a mood to bake today, and there's another whole one in the fridge, besides the one and a half we ate tonight. Believe me, that's plenty for Rick and the kids to plow through."

"Thanks, then. Trip loves cherry pie."

Shayna smiled and her corkscrew curls bounced. "It's like you two have been together forever, you already know each other so well. In case I didn't already tell you, I'm so happy for you I could just scream."

"Thanks." Beth stifled a little twinge of guilt. She and Trip had agreed that the engagement was real, if a bit open-ended. He'd said he loved her, she knew she loved him, she was wearing his grandmother's ring, and he'd showed her off to his entire darned family. So why did she still feel like a giant fraud?

She climbed into the front seat, took the pie from Shayna and set it beside her. "I'll be back at work tomorrow, so I'll see you in town."

"Okay." Shayna stepped back from the car and grinned. "I get to do your hair for the wedding, right?"

"Of course. And be my matron of honor." Where had that come from? She didn't even know for sure there was going to *be* a wedding. But Shayna squealed and bounced.

"Of course! Goodnight. Love you!"

"Love you too, Shay." She closed the door and resisted the urge to bang her forehead on the steering wheel. She drove away from the tree-lined residential street onto the rougher blacktop of a county highway, ignoring the little thrill that she felt when she thought that Trip might be home by now, waiting for her.

She'd gone a couple blocks when Bailey said, "Mommy I think I heard something moving in the back."

"I'm sure it's just road noise, honey." She hadn't left a window open, so it couldn't be a skunk or cat hitching a ride. "We'll be home—I mean back at Mr. Hall's—in a few minutes. Do you want me to turn on the radio?" Damn it, why did she already think of Trip's house as home? And what the heck was Bailey supposed to call him now, anyway?

"Okay."

Beth reached for the stereo knob on the dash board, but before she could push the button, she heard Bailey let loose with an ear-splitting scream.

"Bailey!" Beth felt the vehicle swerve as she instinctively turned to see her child. She forced her eyes back to the road and fought to get the car back under control. Bailey's screams turned into loud, frantic sobs.

"Keep driving."

The voice from behind her was low and menacing. She barely heard it over Bailey's crying. No way was it loud enough to recognize. Knuckles white on the steering wheel, Beth somehow kept the car moving forward.

"I've got a .44 magnum pointed at her little head. If

you don't want this to get real messy, real fast, you'll do exactly as I say."

Nausea twisted Beth's stomach. "W-w-what... Wh-ho...Why..."

"Just drive." The short, harsh bark made her jump, which made the car swerve.

Beth heard herself whimper as she straightened the wheel. Her heart pounded, sweat beaded her forehead, and her mouth had gone totally dry. "P-p-please," she stammered. "Please d-d-don't shoot my daughter. I'll do anything you want."

****

Trevor was getting restless by the time the two men finished eating, so as soon as they were done arguing over the check, Trip stood and moved to lift Trevor from the high chair.

Lawson laid a hand on Trip's arm. "May I?"

Trip nodded and watched as Lawson carefully lifted his nephew and cradled him against his chest.

"Heavy," he grunted. Fierce emotion lurked behind the gray eyes and rugged features, emotion that Trip understood all too well. Even before he'd had Trevor, he's had nieces and nephews, and he'd felt that same powerful sense of familial connection.

"Twenty-nine pounds at his last check-up." Trip hoisted the backpack diaper bag over one shoulder. He hadn't brought a cane, was finally able to leave the house without it, thank God. "He's big for his age, but not outside the normal range. No surprise there, both families tend toward tall. Ahead of the curve on a lot of other development milestones too, though I was beginning to wonder when he'd start walking."

"Yeah, kind of cool to have been there for that." Lawson cradled the child as cautiously as if he were an unexploded bomb as the two men left the café, forcing Trip to smother a smile. The guy had no clue what he was doing, but his instincts weren't half bad.

The evening was a warm one for early June, with a gentle breeze stirring the air. It was late—they'd talked well past the normal dinner hour, and the streetlights cast a warm glow on the quiet town. Drew Lawson leaned one hip against the fender of Trip's SUV and looked around at Main Street.

"Nice place. Reminds me a little of my hometown in Texas."

"It's home," Trip agreed. "There are worse places to raise a kid."

Lawson nodded. "Like Los Angeles."

Trip shrugged. "For some, LA is home. So for them, I guess it works. It wouldn't for me. So Trevor and I came back to Shirley."

"Good for you," Lawson replied. He chucked Trevor's cheek lightly with a knuckle. "Goodbye, Tiger. Uncle Drew will see you soon." He gave the child a tentative hug, then he handed Trevor over to Trip and watched while Trip strapped him into his car seat. The two men shook hands again. Lawson was an all right guy, Trip mused. Too bad his sister hadn't been more like him.

Before Trip could get into the car, his cell phone rang.

"Trip, it's Fitz." His brother spoke in his cold, flat cop voice, and Trip's blood about froze in his veins.

"Now what?" The last time it had been a fire. This time Fitz sounded worse.

There was a short pause, and Trip heard his brother swallow hard before he spoke. "It looks like Beth and Bailey have been—taken."

Chapter Twelve

"What?" Trip didn't care that every person on the street or sidewalk swiveled to see why he'd shouted.

"We found her car. Empty."

"Are you there now?"

"Yeah."

"Where?"

Fitz hesitated.

Trip snarled into the phone. "Where?"

Finally Fitz told him, naming a stretch of rural highway that wouldn't have been too far off of Beth's route home from the Andersons.

"I'm on my way."

"What about Trevor?" Trust Fitz to be the voice of reason.

"Shit!" Trip looked around, his eyes lighting on Drew Lawson. "We're just coming out of Benedetto's. He can spend some quality time with his uncle Drew."

Lawson nodded.

"I hate to say this, but are we sure Lawson didn't have anything to do with this? He did show up in town right about as things started happening to Beth."

True. But Trip looked over at Lawson, whose body had gone on full military alert. The guy looked ready for a fight, but he just didn't seem like a threat to Trip. "He was with me, having dinner. He's clean."

"If you say so. But just so we all feel better, take Trev over to my place, okay? Lily is there with Ree, and they'll keep an eye on him." Lillian Armstrong was a surrogate grandmother to Rhiannon, so it was no surprise she'd been there at dinnertime on a Sunday.

"Done." Trip flipped his phone shut and turned to climb into his car.

"Trouble?" Lawson's voice was low and serious.

Trip nodded. "Somebody kidnapped Beth and Bailey."

He had to fight to get the words out.

Lawson nodded and opened the passenger side door. "Let's go."

Trip wasn't about to argue. He had no doubt whatsoever that the major could hold his own in a fight. He climbed in and gunned the engine as he headed the few blocks to Fitz and Ree's house. He dropped off Trevor, accepted a hug from Ree, and then spun out of the driveway at top speed. Any deputy stupid enough to try to stop him could deal with him tomorrow.

****

About a mile down the dark country highway. Beth's captor told her to turn. A few yards off the highway, she saw another vehicle parked in the underbrush. At the growled instructions of the man in the back of the car, she pulled up behind the dirty brown pick up and turned off her car.

Why hadn't she checked the back end of her station wagon before she and Bailey had gotten in the car? He must have been hidden under the old blanket she kept back there. Who was he, and what did he want? The only glimpse she'd had so far showed he was wearing a ski mask.

"Get out, and get the kid." The gunman's voice sounded familiar now that she could hear it without the car engine. "I'll have my gun on her the whole time, so don't try anything funny."

No, one thing Beth would never, ever, do was take a chance on him hurting Bailey. Slowly and carefully she got out of the car. She left her purse on the seat, alongside the pie. As gently as possible, she closed the front door and opened the back.

"Go on, get her out of that contraption." He'd climbed the seatback and was now next to the car seat, the big black gun waving menacingly in the overhead light. Please God, don't let it go off. Not so close to my baby's head. Beth had to resist the urge to vomit into the weeds beside the car. Only her determination to protect her daughter kept her moving, following instructions.

"Don't cry, baby," she urged as she unbuckled the straps of the car seat. "Hush. You'll make yourself sick."

Once Bailey was in her mother's arms, the child's

sobs quieted a bit. Beth stood stock-still as the man climbed out behind her, then gestured toward the pick up with the hand that wasn't holding the gun. He walked right behind her, then held the gun steady while she climbed into the passenger seat, still holding Bailey.

"Slide over. You're driving."

Obediently, Beth slid into the driver's seat and set Bailey down beside her. She hated leaving her daughter between herself and the gun, but she didn't know what else to do. The bench seat was too far back, she'd have to strain to reach the pedals, but she didn't think trying to move it was a good idea. She did take a second to buckle the middle seatbelt around Bailey, but she didn't bother with her own.

"Let's go." The gunman slammed the door after hoisting himself into the cab. His voice finally dawned on her.

"Len? Len Eliot? Why are you doing this?"

"Just drive!"

The key was in the ignition. Not wanting to make him angry—angrier, anyway, she turned the key and put the truck in gear. "Where to?"

****

Red and blue bubble lights illuminated the night off to the side of the highway. A small, unpaved side road turned off to the right, and Trip saw several official vehicles, including his brother's department SUV. He pulled onto the side road and parked right up behind the sheriff's vehicle. He barely remembered to turn off the engine before he jumped out.

Fitz stood over Beth's station wagon with Jack Stewart, one of his deputies. Several others were combing the surrounding area with flashlights. Lawson was right behind Trip when he strode up to his brother.

"Well?"

Fitz shrugged. "About fifteen minutes ago, one of my deputies was driving by and saw the abandoned car. He stopped to check it out. Since her purse is still in the car, with her cell phone and wallet inside, he got real suspicious. No woman would leave that voluntarily. Plus there's the pie and the keys are still in the ignition.

"There's no blood, or signs of a fight, on the other

hand, which is good. Looks like somebody may have hid under the blanket in back. We've got the state police crime lab guys on the way to look for hairs or whatever.

"Shit."

Fitz nodded. "Looks like there was another vehicle—something bigger like a truck or SUV parked right ahead. It took off down this road. After that, we have no clue. Any idea where she was going, or what time?"

"She was at Rick and Shayna Anderson's house for dinner. They'd know when she left."

Fitz spoke into his radio. "Doris will give Shayna a call. She's better at the people stuff than I am."

Trip nodded. Fitz's secretary/dispatcher was an institution in the town. She'd get the job done.

"Anything I can do, Sheriff?" Drew Lawson spoke up from beside Trip.

"Lawson." Fitz practically spit the name. "Yeah, you can tell me where you were this evening."

"I told you he was with me," Trip interjected. "At Benedetto's. Since about six o'clock."

Lawson nodded. "I know you've got no reason to believe me, but I had nothing to do with this. If I thought my nephew was in a bad situation, I might have done something to him—" He jerked his head toward Trip. "But I'd never go after innocents. Not my style. Anyway, I've got some training in night ops if you need something."

Fitz raised one eyebrow. "Just what did you do for Uncle Sam all these years?"

Trip answered for him. "Sniper." When Drew swiveled to look at him, he just shrugged. "What can I say? Your sister liked to brag."

Lawson shook his head. Then he looked up at Fitz. "You got scent hounds around here? Sometimes they can follow a vehicle."

Fitz nodded. "Gil Henderson's getting his bloodhounds over here ASAP."

Trip saw something off in the distance and gulped. *No. No way. Couldn't be.*

He tapped his brother on the shoulder.

"What?"

Instead of replying, Trip just pointed. Fitz looked over at the county highway, bobbled his radio, and swore under his breath.

"So you see her too?"

"Oh yeah."

"You think..." Trip's mouth was too dry to finish the sentence.

"It's her." Fitz answered like he knew what he was talking about. Trip filed that away to ask about later.

"Should we follow her?" Trip had to swallow hard, but he got the words out.

"What the hell are you two talking about?" Lawson's testy voice broke into the conversation.

Fitz pointed to the road. "You see anything over there?"

He nodded. "She somebody you know?"

Fitz snorted. "You could say that. Look closely at her feet." He reached into his SUV and pulled out his rifle.

"What the hell?" Lawson was still staring at the woman in white.

"They don't—they don't quite touch the ground, do they?" Trip stuttered. He had never heard that particular detail about the family ghost. But he looked over at the Native American woman. She had long black braids and wore a white fringed dress and shawl. Sure enough, her moccasin-covered feet hovered just a few inches above the graveled surface of the shoulder of the road.

"Looks like she wants us to follow," Trip said.

The woman pointed to his SUV and nodded.

"What the hell is going on here?"

Lawson's tone was annoyed and impatient—maybe even a little scared. None of the other deputies in the area seemed to notice the woman at all.

Fitz yelled, "Be right back," to one of his deputies, then moved to Trip's SUV and climbed in the passenger side even as Trip was getting into the driver's seat. Lawson got into the back without missing a beat.

While Trip spun the truck around toward the woman in white, Fitz turned to Lawson. "Looks like you've been adopted," he said levelly. "Meet Singing Bird. The Hall family ghost."

****

Beth pulled the truck behind the tiny shack as Len instructed, willing her hands not to shake or her teeth to chatter. The place looked deserted, and she wasn't at all sure where they were. She'd been too scared to really keep track of which back road he'd ordered her down. Bailey had stopped sobbing. Now she just huddled next to Beth in a terrified heap.

Len opened his door and stood, never letting the gun waver away from Beth or Bailey. "You get out now," he told Beth. "Move nice and slow, and keep your hands where I can see them."

She was shaking so badly her knees barely held her up, but she did as he said. She reached into the cab for Bailey, but stopped when Len waved the gun.

"Up on the porch," he ordered.

When Beth stepped onto the narrow wooden stoop, he reached into the cab and hauled Bailey out by her arm. Bailey started crying again, and wrested her arm away so forcefully, Beth was terrified he'd pull the tiny limb out of its socket. She lunged toward her daughter, but was brought up short by another deadly cold glare from Len. She bit her knuckle to keep from screaming at him until he pushed Bailey ahead of him toward the stoop.

"Inside."

Beth pushed open the door to what was obviously an old abandoned line shack. There were ranchlands out here that hadn't been in use for years—this had to be one of them. Lit only by a pair of camp lanterns, the room was about ten by fifteen feet, with a door on one end that probably led to a bathroom. An ancient cook top was set in a counter on one end, along with a metal sink. A small opening beneath the counter might have once held a half-sized refrigerator. A set of metal bunk beds and a battered wooden dinette set were the only furnishings in the place. The bottom bed had a green sleeping bag unrolled across it.

"Sit on the bed," Len told Beth. "And give me your hand." He finally tugged the ski mask off over his head and tossed it on the table.

She sat. Bailey ran and hugged Beth's knee. Her nose was running and tears dripped down her precious face. Beth lifted her hand to wipe them away, but Len grabbed it and wrenched it to the side, up against the metal post holding up the top bunk. He gestured with the gun in his other hand.

"Hold it there."

Beth nodded and flattened her other hand on Bailey's back, holding her close. Len reached in the back pocket of his jeans and pulled out a pair of handcuffs. With a few rough movements, he cuffed Beth's right hand to the bed frame.

Bailey stared at something on the other side of the room, then nodded her head. Hopefully there wasn't a snake or a bat in the building. Beth looked, but saw nothing in the shadows. Len finished testing the cuffs, then nodded and stepped back. He scowled, as though he wasn't quite sure what to do next.

"It's okay Mommy," Bailey whispered. "Daddy will be here soon to save us."

Beth didn't know if her daughter believed that Daniel was an angel who would swoop to the rescue, or if she meant Trip. She just wished she had half as much faith that either one of them would be coming.

Len sneered. "You don't have a daddy. Now shut up!"

"But I gotta go potty," Bailey whined. She squeezed her knees together and looked up at Len with big pitiful eyes.

"What?" He seemed intent on his thoughts until interrupted by her plaints.

"I gotta use the potty." Her tiny face scrunched up tight.

Len frowned.

Bailey wriggled more. "Please."

Len glowered for a moment then nodded toward the wooden door in the far wall. "In there. Don't try anything."

Bailey ran into the bathroom and slammed the door. Len stared hard at Beth until she felt her skin crawl. "Now that we're alone..."

****

"What the hell do you mean ghost?"

"Ghost." Fitz grunted the response. "Dead person. Floats above the ground. Seems to like going for help when someone in our family is in trouble."

"Like their car is in a ditch in the snow, maybe?" Trip asked. He was intent on following the figure that was now—there was no other way to describe it—*flying* down the road ahead of them.

"Yeah, like that," Fitz agreed grumpily.

So Trip had been right about Ree's car crash last spring. Singing Bird had brought Fitz to the rescue. Damn.

"No fucking way." Lawson stared ahead. "She's goddamn flying!"

"Guess ghosts can do that," Trip replied.

"And only family can supposedly see her," Fitz added. "But you did. Weird."

"Figure that means we were supposed to bring him," Trip added.

"Maybe." Fitz didn't sound convinced, but he wasn't pissed either. "I'm not gonna ask her, are you?"

"Nope."

When Singing Bird stopped and held up a hand, Trip pulled the SUV off onto the shoulder and cut the engine. All three men got out. Fitz looked at Lawson. "Sniper, huh?"

Lawson nodded grimly.

"Here." Fitz handed him the rifle, then turned to Trip. "Your leg up to this?"

"What do you think?" Trip glared. "If it was Ree who was missing? Or your kid?"

Fitz nodded. "I'd crawl if I had to." He drew his back-up pistol, a 22 caliber snub nose from his ankle holster and handed it to Trip. Then he pulled his service weapon from his shoulder holster. "Lock and load, boys."

They followed the ghost down a side road, through a woodlot. At the edge of the grove, Trip saw what looked like an abandoned line shack. The soft glow of candles or firelight filtered out the single narrow window.

"I think we're on the old Garrison property," Fitz whispered. "Been vacant about three years now."

"So anyone could have picked it as a hideout." Trip let his brother lead, picking his footing carefully to spare his damned gimpy leg.

Their guide motioned them around to the back of the shack. Sure enough, there was a pick up parked beside the shack. On one end of this side was another window. While they watched, that window slowly opened, and a tiny head, topped with gold curls appeared. Bailey seemed to be struggling to reach the sill, so without thinking, Trip ran over to lift her and pull her out.

"Daddy!" she squealed. Her small hands clutched at his hair as he tried to wriggle her out the small opening in the glass. She was in a tiny bathroom, with no lights, and had obviously stood on the toilet tank to climb up to the window. It was a miracle she hadn't fallen.

A loud roar split the night and Trip saw the door leading to the main room of the shack shake as if someone was rattling it to get in.

"You locked it? Good girl."

Bailey nodded, her little butt wriggling through the open pane. Before he could move aside, Trip heard a gunshot and the door between the rooms burst open.

"Down, Hall!"

"Hold on, short stuff, Daddy's got you." Pulling Bailey with him, Trip rolled to the ground, just as another face appeared at the window. He heard something in his knee go pop, then the rifle cracked off to his left, away from the house. There was a scream then a thud from inside the bathroom. Over it all he heard Beth from somewhere inside the shack, frantically screaming Bailey's name.

Chapter Thirteen

Len Eliot wasn't dead.

"I know that pulling the shot was absolutely against protocol," Drew Lawson admitted later, sipping the thick black sludge that passed for coffee in the sheriff's office.

He seemed to have bonded with the Hall brothers tonight. Beth was grateful enough to him for shooting Eliot that she wasn't about to quibble about how he'd gotten it done. "But—I've done so much killing in the last few years—I just couldn't do it again. Not when I could take out his gun arm instead."

"No complaints from me," Fitz replied. "Lot less paperwork that way." Eliot would probably never have full use of his right arm again, the EMT's had told them, but he'd survive. Which was more than he'd deserved, in Beth's opinion. Judging from his ranting and raving as the EMT's had taken him away, he'd be spending the next several years in a mental institution

Fitz sat in his office chair, feet kicked up on top of the metal desk. The others were clustered around him—Trip and Beth in the two guest chairs, pushed as close together as they could manage, and Lawson parked on top of a file cabinet. Trip's foot was up on an overturned trash can, with an ice pack on his bad knee. Bailey sat on his other leg, her arms around his neck, her face buried in his shoulder. She hadn't let go of him for long since he'd pulled her out that window. Beth tried not to be jealous. Not that she minded her daughter holding onto the man she now insisted on calling Daddy. Beth didn't mind that a bit. No, she minded that there was no room on Trip's lap for her.

Bailey had let Beth hold her for a while after they'd gotten her uncuffed from those damned metal bunk beds, but as soon as they were in the car on the way out of that hell hole, she'd been back in Trip's lap. Of course, he'd kept Beth pressed up against him on the other side. He was the one who hadn't been able to let go of her, which made Beth's heart soar. She knew his knee had to hurt like hell, but he'd refused to go to the hospital. Somehow, she couldn't bring herself to insist. It felt too damn good just to be with him, now, after being afraid she'd never see him again.

"I told the bad man my daddy was going to save us," Bailey insisted. "The white lady told me so. Right 'fore she told me to climb out the window."

"White lady?" Beth asked. "Who..."

"It's a long story, Beth..." Trip began.

"I told you before, Mommy." Bailey shook her head. "My garden angel. The same one who told me about the fire."

"I think guardian angel is as good an explanation as any," Fitz agreed. "Though she's going down in the reports as 'anonymous tip.' We all agreed on that?"

The men all nodded. Beth knew they were keeping something from her, but when Trip murmured, "I'll explain when we get home, okay?" she sighed her agreement. Home. She'd never doubt again that wherever Trip was, that was home. For Beth and for Bailey as well.

"So one more time for the report, Beth. Tell me what Len Eliot said to you in the line shack." Fitz hit the button on the tape recorder in front of him. Trip started to object, but Beth squeezed his hand and shook her head.

"It's okay, honey. I can do this."

Trip nodded, so Beth spoke slowly and carefully toward the mike.

"He said I was supposed to be his. He thought I was playing hard to get, but that was okay, he didn't mind taking his time. But then I started going out with Trip—he may have phrased that a little differently—and he knew he had to take matters into his own hands. When he heard about the engagement, he said it was time to take back what was rightly his. So he followed me to Shayna's and waited. He didn't expect me to have Bailey, but he figured he could use her to make me "see reason" and do what he wanted." She drew in a ragged, shuddering breath, remembering how Len had used her daughter as a hostage.

"You're doing great, Beth." Fitz's voice was the same warm tone he'd use for any of his sisters, and that warmed Beth's heart, too. She felt surrounded by love and family now in a way she hadn't since her parents had been alive.

"He was going to keep us there," Beth added. "He wasn't—wasn't sane at all, was he?"

"No," Fitz told her. "Just your garden variety sociopath. They've matched up his fingerprints to the ones found at your apartment, so he's going to do time for the arson as well as the kidnapping."

Beth buried her face in Trip's shoulder for a moment, felt the warm, solid strength of him, smelled his sweaty, masculine scent, overlain with the dirt and pine needles he'd rolled in to protect Bailey. "Poor Mr. Eliot," she murmured. "Len was his only son."

"His daughter and her husband are coming to help him out." Rhiannon entered the office, carrying Trevor. Beth immediately reached for the toddler at the same time as Trip held out the hand that wasn't holding Bailey. With a soft smile, he let Beth take Trevor, then he wrapped his long, strong arm around them both, and leaned his cheek on the top of Beth's head.

"Thank goodness you're okay." Ree leaned down and kissed Bailey's head, then gave Beth a gentle hug. "I hear you had a little help from a certain lady in white," she said to Bailey.

"My garden angel," Bailey agreed.

"Yep." Ree tapped the little girl's cheek, and winked at Beth. "I think we share the same one, kiddo. We'll have to compare notes sometime."

"I think there's something in the air in this town." Lawson growled. "Not only are all of you bug-nuts, but you've made me crazy as well."

Fitz nodded. "You're probably right. Welcome to Shirley."

****

"Goodnight, sweetheart. You need to go to sleep now." Trip wasn't sure who he was trying to convince, Bailey or himself. Both he and Beth sat on the edge of the bed, trying to force themselves to let go of their daughter so she could go to sleep.

"Uh-huh. 'Night Mommy. 'Night Daddy. The white lady says you can go to bed now. I'll be okay."

Trip looked around. He didn't see the ghost, but hell, that didn't mean she wasn't here. He'd seen her when he needed her. That's all that mattered.

"Okay." Beth kissed Bailey goodnight, then stood, and handed Trip his cane.

It galled him to admit it, but he'd need it for a few days, along with a knee brace. He'd sprained it, nothing more, but it hurt like hell. Still, it was more than worth any amount of pain to have gotten his little angel out that window. He kissed Bailey once last time then stood and followed Beth from the room. He turned off the overhead light as he left, but they left the hall light on, and both the kids' bedroom doors open. Gonzo thumped his tail, but remained behind, the three-legged sentinel in Bailey's room.

"Let's get you into bed, mister," Beth said, wrapping her arm around his waist as they moved down the hallway. "Once we're sure Bailey's asleep, my hero can get his reward."

"I got that the minute I saw that you were both all right." He moved into the bedroom and sat down on the bed. He'd changed into sweats when they got home to accommodate the knee brace, kept the knee up and on ice while Beth and Bailey both took a hot bubble bath to cleanse away some of the dirt and horror of the evening. Now standing before him in a tank top and stretchy shorts, Beth was the most beautiful sight he'd ever seen.

"I believe you." She smiled crookedly from across the room. "In case I've been remiss in saying it, I love you, Howard Hemingway Hall. For a little while there tonight I wasn't sure I'd ever get the chance to tell you that."

Trip felt his eyes water up. He opened his arms, felt a huge load of ice lift off his heart when she sauntered over and stepped into them. "I love you, Beth. Forever and always. I was afraid I'd lost you tonight, and the world would have never been the same again."

"But you didn't. You saved us." She pressed kisses on his cheeks.

"Well, I had some help." He chuckled as she pushed him back onto the bed then straddled him with her knees, staring down at him, her expression fierce and loving.

"Yes, you did. And I'm not sure how much or from where. But that doesn't matter. Bailey and I needed you, and you were there for us."

"I'll always be there for you, honey. I wish you could believe that." He prayed that he'd someday be able to break down the wall around her heart and earn her trust.

Then she smiled and it was like the sun coming out.

"I do."

"You do?"

"I trust you, Trip. With my life. With my daughter's. Most of all with my heart."

"Beth—" The words stuck in his throat. She was offering him the world on a plate.

"You asked me this once, and I was too chicken to say yes. So this time I'm asking you. Will you marry me, Trip? Will you spend the rest of your life with me, laughing with me, putting up with my moods, raising our children? Loving me?"

He was too choked up to speak, so he just looked into her big brown eyes and nodded. When he saw two fat tears welling up in the coffee-colored depths, he gripped her arms and rolled, flipping them both so that he was on top. It hurt his knee a bit, but he couldn't have cared less. He swallowed hard and managed to speak.

"I. Love. You." He kissed her lips between each word. "I want to marry you as soon as we can arrange it. That okay with you?"

She nodded and smiled. He kissed away the twin tears that dripped down her cheeks.

"And I want you to adopt Trevor, and I'm *going* to adopt Bailey. That okay too?"

She nodded again.

"And we'll spend the rest of our lives making up for the fourteen years we wasted by not being together. Got it?"

"Got it." She reached up and wiped a tear he hadn't noticed escaping his own eyes. "I love you, Trip. Have all my life."

"Then it's about freaking time I got things right. I may be a little slow, Beth. But you know how you keep saying, once a cowboy, always a cowboy? One thing I remember from my junior rodeo days—I know how to hang on, and never let go."

She laughed—her musical yet dorky laugh, and it was the most beautiful, sexiest sound on Earth. "Hmmm—think your knee's up for a ride, cowboy? I bet you can last a good eight seconds."

"With you? Maybe, maybe not. But I've got a better idea, darlin'. I think this time, it's the cowgirl's turn to ride."

Epilogue

It was Christmas at the Crazy H. All the kids were clustered on the floor while their parents perched on sofas and chairs around the living room. Singing Bird and her husband Jack looked down on the family from their perch at the top of the stairs.

"We did good with this bunch, didn't we, sweet cheeks?"

Singing Bird nodded. She winked down at Rhiannon and little Bailey, the only two who could see them except in emergencies, and turned back to her husband. Ree had coached her niece about admitting to seeing ghosts in public, so Bailey just winked back and turned away. Her attention was on her favorite present anyway.

"Mommy, can I hold Brenna?" She looked up at her ten-day-old sister who was sleeping in Beth's lap. Little Brenna had been quite the surprise to her parents, who had accepted that their family was complete with two children. Singing Bird didn't think Trip had stopped grinning since the day the pregnancy was confirmed.

"Not now, sweetie," Trip admonished with a hug. "Later on, after her nap. Right now, why don't you get that big green package, and give it to Harry?"

Bailey obediently handed the present to her three-year old cousin, and then the red one just like it to his twin brother Jack.

Singing Bird smiled at her husband. "Little Jack sure does have your eyes. Nice of Ree to name him after you." Ree and Fitz had their hands full with the rambunctious twins, not to mention their baby sister.

Crazy Jack, as he'd been known in his lifetime, grunted. "Better yet that they named the little girl for you." Fitz and Ree's one-year old daughter was called Anne Singing Bird Hall. Right now she was sharing a blanket with CJ and Allie's youngest boy Jamie, while three-year-old Tom played trucks with four-year-old Trevor in the corner. The house was packed to the gills, and no one was happier about that than the two ghosts who watched over the gathering.

"We're gonna have our hands full with this next batch." Jack remarked, a pleased grin on his face. "They're gonna keep a couple of old ghosts on their toes."

"Oh, I think we're up to it." Singing Bird snuggled up to his waist and leaned her head on his shoulder. "We do a pretty good job for a couple of old 'garden angels'."

A word about the author...

Cindy Spencer Pape has been, among other things, a banker, a teacher, and an elected politician, though she swears she got better. She currently works in environmental education, when she can fit it in around writing. She lives in Michigan with her husband, two teenage sons, a dog, a lizard, and various other small creatures, all of which are easier to clean up after than the three male humans.

Visit Cindy at www.cindyspencerpape.com

Printed in the United States
126949LV00001BA/61-72/P